MONTANA MAVERICKS

Welcome to Big Sky Country! Where spirited men and women discover love on the range.

LEGACY OF TENACITY

As the town begins to heal from its scars and scandals, its single cowboys (and cowgirls) are ready for a fresh start. They know that love can grow in the most unexpected places and that down doesn't mean out. So make a wish on a Montana moon for all to be revealed—they've waited for their sweethearts long enough!

COUNTING ON A MAVERICK

Rancher Grayson Abernathy knows that JenniLynn Garrett is special from the moment he meets her. But she's also fresh off a divorce and not looking to start over with someone else. He convinces himself they can keep their relationship platonic. But the more time they spend together, the more he realizes he doesn't want to be "just friends"... He wants forever.

Dear Reader,

Welcome to Tenacity, Montana! I had so much fun writing this Montana Mavericks story about single parents and their adorable—and sometimes mischievous—children.

In the past year, JenniLynn Garrett has gone from being a stay-at-home married mother of three girls to a divorcée and the mayor of Tenacity. Grayson Abernathy is a wealthy rancher and autism coach. He teams up with JenniLynn to start a job program for the neurodivergent population. Grayson's young son is with him for the summer, and Grayson and JenniLynn's business meetups quickly become playdates that include lots of puppies.

Their attraction is palpable, but romance is the last thing on JenniLynn's mind. At least, it was. In moments of weakness, she daydreams about a perfectly blended family.

I hope you enjoy *Counting on a Maverick*. As always, thank you so much for reading one of my books!

Best wishes,

Makenna Lee

COUNTING ON
A MAVERICK

MAKENNA LEE

MONTANA MAVERICKS

Special thanks and acknowledgment are given to Makenna Lee for her contribution to the Montana Mavericks: Legacy of Tenacity miniseries.

Recycling programs for this product may not exist in your area.

ISBN-13: 978-1-335-54092-8

Counting on a Maverick

Harlequin Enterprises ULC
22 Adelaide St. West, 41st Floor
Toronto, Ontario M5H 4E3, Canada
www.Harlequin.com

HarperCollins Publishers
Macken House, 39/40 Mayor Street Upper,
Dublin 1, D01 C9W8, Ireland
www.HarperCollins.com

Printed in Lithuania

1 2 3 4 5 6 7 8 9 10 LIT 28 27 26 25

Makenna Lee is an award-winning romance author living in the Texas Hill Country with her real-life hero and their two children, one of whom has Down syndrome and inspired her first Harlequin book, *A Sheriff's Star*. She writes heartwarming contemporary romance that celebrates real-life challenges and the power of love and acceptance. She has been known to make people laugh and cry in the same book. Makenna is often drinking coffee with a cat on her lap while writing, reading or plotting a new story. Her wish is to write stories that touch your heart, making you feel, think and dream.

Books by Makenna Lee

Montana Mavericks: Legacy of Tenacity

Counting on a Maverick

Harlequin Special Edition

The Cameron Family

Her Cowboy for the Holiday
Stranded with the Cowboy

The Women of Dalton Ranch

The Rancher's Love Song
Her Secret to Keep
Her New Year's Wish List

Home to Oak Hollow

A Sheriff's Star
In the Key of Family
A Child's Christmas Wish
A Marriage of Benefits
Lessons in Fatherhood

Visit the Author Profile page
at Harlequin.com for more titles.

For David.
It's been a joy to watch you raise an amazing daughter.

Chapter One

Grayson Abernathy approached the door of the mayor's private office. It was partially open, and he could see Mayor Garrett as she rummaged through a pink purse on her desk. Her blond hair fell forward around her shoulders, and her pretty heart-shaped face was set in concentration. She wasn't aware of him standing there, so he raised a fist to knock on the doorframe.

"Spit fire and save matches!" said Mayor JenniLynn Garrett.

Grayson bit back a chuckle at her creative cursing and lowered his hand.

Her wallet had a bright red, half-eaten lollipop stuck to the pink leather. She pried it loose with a slow sigh that he recognized as a sign of an exhausted parent, but with a straightening of her spine, her expression changed to one of determination. Considering the year she'd had, he admired her strength and grit. He'd heard the stories and seen her around town, and although they'd never officially met, he'd noticed her every time. He found himself suddenly impatient to get to know her.

"Good afternoon, Mayor Garrett."

She sucked in a sharp breath and slapped a hand to her

heart. Unfortunately, it was the one holding the candy. "Oh, my gosh. Mr. Abernathy, I didn't see you there."

He took off his Stetson and held it against his chest in the way old cowboys had taught him to do when greeting a lady. "Sorry to startle you. It looks like you're in a bit of a sticky situation."

She groaned, peeled the red candy from her white blouse and dropped it into a trash can. "My two-year-old has a tendency to save her partially eaten treats for later, and unfortunately, it's occasionally in my purse without my knowledge."

"I once had to make a trip to the barber because of a chewing gum incident." Grayson rubbed a hand through his short, light brown hair and then put on his cowboy hat.

"Oh, no. I've thankfully managed to avoid that catastrophe."

"I can go wait somewhere else if you need some time before the meeting." He hooked a thumb back toward the hallway.

"Oh, no, I'm so sorry. Please, come in. It's nice to officially meet you, Mr. Abernathy. I would shake your hand but..." She wiggled her sticky fingers.

"No worries. Please, call me Grayson."

The way her lips moved, he thought she'd say his name, and for some reason he really wanted to hear it. Instead, she opened a desk drawer and grabbed a packet of wet wipes.

"Have a seat while I tend to this mess." The plastic crinkled as she fished out one of the wet cloths.

He chose a chair at a small conference table near the windows that looked out over Central Avenue, but he found her more entertaining as she meticulously cleaned her hands. Her fingers were long and narrow and tipped with short nails neatly painted one of those neutral colors professional women seemed to stick to.

"I hesitate to investigate the rest of the inside of my purse." She pulled out another wipe and dabbed at the spot on her blouse. "I've become a good multitasker, but I think I'll save that chore for later."

"There are some things that can wait," he agreed.

"I try to tell myself that all the time. I can be a bit of an overachiever."

Grayson could see that about her. She would have to be a go-getter to do her job all while being a single mom. "Sounds like the kind of person I want running my town."

Her smile was broad, highlighting her heart-shaped face and blue eyes. He admired her strength and tenacity, which was very fitting since it was the name of the town she was running. She'd lived through the scandal of having her own husband caught ballot tampering in the mayoral election. The wildest part was that it had *not* been in her favor. Her own husband had bet against her, and Grayson thought she'd made a wise decision by divorcing the fool.

She didn't let the whispers get her down, or if they did, she didn't let it show, but her emotions were no doubt still tender. Her ex-husband was awaiting his trial, and he couldn't imagine having something like that hanging over him.

"Brent and Barrett should be here any minute," he said.

She joined him at the conference table. "I'm glad you got here first. I want to personally thank you for being such a generous donor to The Tenacity Dinosaur Center and Park."

"I'm happy to do it. I became a donor because of the dinosaur bones that were discovered in the area. Finding a piece of the long-ago past should excite everyone."

She looked right at him with a grin. "We're lucky to have found someone with a childlike love for dinosaurs."

For a brief moment, he thought she was teasing him about being a silly boy who likes dinosaurs, but then she continued.

"I still have my little plastic dinosaurs from when I was a kid," she said. "Now, my girls play with them."

Grayson's smile returned. "Oh, yeah? I don't know what happened to mine."

"As a kid I never imagined real dinosaur fossils would be discovered in my little Montana town. Now our Dinosaur Center is open and attracting visitors from all over. It will change the future of Tenacity. I've been working closely with them, and it should bring in much-needed income for the town. I would love to be the mayor who delivers a prosperous future."

"I hope to be one of the people who helps you with that. Any news on the Bruckner brothers who claim to own the land?"

"It's still an ongoing investigation."

Grayson glanced at the antique pendulum clock on top of a bookcase, curious if it had always been in the office or if such an antique belonged to her. He liked clocks and had a small collection, but he didn't have anything like this one. "Did that clock come with the mayor's office?"

"No. It's mine," she said proudly. "It belonged to my grandmother, and I brought it with me to remind me every day about the lessons she taught me."

Before he could be nosey and ask her about those lessons, the other two men could be heard talking as they neared her office. Since Brent Woodson and Barrett Deroy had started The Tenacity Foundation to restore the town to its former glory, there had been real progress. Grayson was impressed with what they had accomplished, and he was happy he had the means to help.

"Welcome, gentlemen," said Mayor JenniLynn Garrett.

"Thank you all for meeting here so we can explore how Tenacity can better serve our autistic population."

"Happy to be here." Brent said.

The way Brent's eyes cut around the room, Grayson wasn't so sure his cousin Sage's fiancé was happy to be in this particular space. Once upon a time, it had been his father's office, and being here no doubt brought up memories of another scandal from years ago.

He greeted Barrett, and then while the mayor and Barrett spoke on one side of the room, he quietly asked Brent about his cousin. "What's Sage up to?"

"She's looking forward to seeing your son and doing some baking," Brent said. "When do you get Adam from his mother?"

"In just a few days. I can't wait to have him with me again." Summers and vacations weren't enough, and he hated missing the everyday moments. He missed reading stories to him before bed when his hair was damp from his bath and he smelled like soap. He missed watching his son fall asleep, knowing that he was under the same roof and could keep him safe throughout the night.

"Would anyone like a cup of coffee or hot tea?" the mayor asked as she walked over to a kitchenette area in one corner with a coffeepot and mini refrigerator. "I just brewed a fresh pot. I also have cold drinks."

"I would like coffee, please," Grayson said.

Once they were all seated with their beverages, she straightened the pad and three different colored pens in front of her and smiled at him. "Mr. Abernathy, would you tell us more about your ideas?"

"I volunteer as a job coach for teens and adults who are on the spectrum, and I would like to start a program that will help autistic adults find lasting employment in the town. But for it to be truly successful, I propose having a bootcamp of sorts to help clients feel more comfortable, and to help employers to understand what to expect. It would hopefully be a way to give everyone the tools they need for success."

"I love this idea." The mayor started writing on her pad with a magenta pen.

"Do you have clients ready to work?" Barrett asked.

"Several, and more that will be ready soon," Grayson said. "Getting the community involved will help make it a greater success."

Brent leaned back in his chair. "I agree. How do you see the bootcamp working?"

"That's what I'm hoping all of you can help me work out. My clients typically need support to thrive in the workforce, or sometimes it's just about educating the employers. So if there's a plan in place, both parties benefit."

Mayor Garrett took notes—using three different colors of ink—while they all brainstormed ideas. Grayson shared more about how he worked with the teens and adults to prepare them for jobs, and that spurred more ideas. The whole time, he had to keep reminding himself not to stare at the pretty woman across from him.

Tapping her turquoise pen, she studied her notes. "I need to look into the funding," she said.

"I can help with that, too," Grayson said. "I'm on the board of a special needs foundation, and they will be able to help us out with this program."

"Excellent news." The mayor twirled a lock of her blond hair around her finger but then seemed to realize what she was doing and flipped the shiny strands away from her face as if trying to break the habit. "Mr. Abernathy, how did you become so knowledgeable about autism?"

"My sixteen-year-old nephew, Oscar, is autistic, and he

sparked my desire to learn about and to help support the autistic community."

"Do you have a name for the program you'd like to start here?" the town's distractingly pretty mayor asked him.

"What do you think about Tenacity Job Corps?"

"I like it," she said, and the other men agreed.

"Simple and to the point," Barrett said.

JenniLynn's interest in the program he championed was genuine, and Grayson appreciated this. He had not expected this to be so easy. He wasn't only getting cooperation, he was getting enthusiasm. "I think we are already off to a great start with this program."

She placed all three ink pens neatly beside the tablet. "Do you think my office might be a good place for one of your clients to work? I need to hire a new secretary."

From what he'd observed about her and her office so far, Grayson thought it might be the perfect place. "We should definitely discuss that once our meeting is done."

"I think we've covered everything we need to," Brent said and grinned at Grayson in a way that told him he'd noticed his eagerness to hang around.

The mayor stood. "Thank you all for meeting today and for being so excited to make our town a great place for everyone to live."

Brent and Barrett said their goodbyes and left, but Grayson stayed behind to discuss someone working in her office.

"Are you looking for a full- or part-time employee?"

"Full-time. My last secretary went on maternity leave and loves being a mom so much she has decided to stay home with her sweet baby boy."

Before they could discuss anything more, the door swung open, and a little girl ran into the office.

"Mommy, I'm here!"

"Hi, Sasha." JenniLynn's narrow, conservative skirt and high heels didn't stop her from kneeling on the wooden floor and opening her arms to welcome her little girl into a hug. She straightened the blonde braids that hung over each of Sasha's shoulders. "Did you have a good day?"

"I was very good."

She said it in a way that made Grayson think this might not always be the case.

Sasha switched to a loud whisper. "But I did have to sit in the quiet zone for five minutes."

Before she could respond to her daughter's announcement, two more carbon copies of JenniLynn came through the doorway followed by a young woman who must be their babysitter. The woman waved to the mayor and made her exit. One child was a few years older than Sasha and had long hair even more pale than her mother's. She was holding the hand of a toddler with ringlets bouncing around her head.

The three girls almost knocked their mother over with their enthusiastic hugs and there was lots of giggling. He was warmed by the sweet sight. Grayson found himself smiling at the scene, but it also made his heart ache for such a daily greeting. He really missed his son and was counting the hours until he saw him.

Grayson was excited about starting a new phase of his life in Tenacity. His cattle had arrived in several eighteen wheelers and were settling in on his Ambling Hills Ranch, where there was plenty of grass, shade and fresh water. It was taking him a little longer to settle into the big empty house.

Sasha popped a hand over her mouth and then pointed a tiny finger at him. "Mommy, there's a man in here."

"Girls, this is Mr. Abernathy." She wobbled on her high

heels for only a moment as she stood and then smiled at him. "This is my oldest daughter, Lila."

"Hi," Lila said shyly and leaned into her mother's side.

"I'm Sasha," said the one with braids. "I'm four. How old are you, Mr. Ab…? What's your name again?"

He grinned. "You can call me Mr. Grayson."

"Sasha, it's not nice to ask grownups their age," the mayor said to her daughter.

The little girl put her hands on her hips. "But everyone is always asking me."

He couldn't help but chuckle. "I'm old. I'm forty, and it's very nice to meet all of you."

JenniLynn looked over her shoulder at the toddler hiding behind her. "Hallie, honey, come say hello to Mr. Grayson."

The toddler peeked around her hip and stared at his feet, but she didn't say a word.

Lila reached over to pat her little sister's head. "Hallie doesn't really like strangers."

Grayson smiled in a way he hoped was comforting. "That's okay. I completely understand."

"You girls go pick a snack and then sit at the table while I finish my business with Mr. Grayson. There are apple slices and cheese sticks."

As the girls clustered around the mini fridge, the two of them moved to her desk, and he sat in the leather chair across from her.

"Sorry about all the questions. I don't know how much you know, but it's been a rough year for my girls," she said quietly. "Sasha is acting out and the other two have their own things going on."

"I've heard enough about the past year to know that their acting out is understandable. It is also obvious that you're a good mom."

"I do my best."

"Mommy, Hallie spilled her orange juice," Sasha announced.

JenniLynn sighed and gave him a withering smile. "Lila, please grab some paper towels. I'll be there in just a minute."

"Why don't I get out of your way. It looks like it's time for me to let you switch into your mommy role without me being a distraction."

"I appreciate your understanding."

"Can we set up another meeting to talk more about a job opportunity for someone here at your office and the Job Corps bootcamp?"

"Absolutely." She looked at her large desktop calendar that had things neatly written in different colored ink. "Can you meet on Thursday afternoon about two?"

"That works for me," he said.

"Thank you again for understanding."

"Of course." They exchanged phone numbers and then he prepared to take his leave. "Goodbye, girls."

Lila returned his wave, Sasha shouted a goodbye and Hallie ducked down so only her eyes could be seen above the tabletop. Before he closed the door behind himself, his last glimpse was of the pretty mayor who intrigued him more than anyone had in a long time.

He would have to keep reminding himself that she was a single mom with a demanding job, and especially the fact that she was recently divorced and likely had a wounded heart.

Chapter Two

Backpacks were hung on their hooks and little pink and purple shoes were lined up in the mudroom. JenniLynn Garrett kicked off her high heels, turned on the radio and opened a bottle of sparkling water before collapsing onto one of the stools at her long kitchen island. Switching roles from running a town to running a household as a single mother of three required a few essential calming habits to recharge before she could shift into full mommy mode. Then she would turn to the task of preparing a dinner that everyone would eat.

Sasha was still full of energy, and with her arms outstretched, she spun in a circle in the middle of the connected family room. Hallie was on the floor getting her zoo animals out of a basket one at a time and lining them in a neat row along the transition of the hardwood kitchen floor to the carpeted family room.

She sipped her drink and smiled at her two youngest. She loved being a mom. It gave her a sense of purpose and filled up her heart, but she also liked waking up every morning with the challenge of making her community a better place for her family to live. Her colleagues at Town Hall seemed to appreciate her, and women often stopped her on the street and congratulated her for breaking the "glass ceiling" and being the first female mayor of Tenacity. Much of her job involved common sense, and JenniLynn's lack of political experience was rather a plus. Although she did butt heads with members of the town council from time to time.

But…there was always a sense of guilt about being a working mom. An added pressure she put upon herself.

After all the scandal her husband had caused with his scheming and ballot tampering, she also felt the need to prove herself and make up for the trouble that had come along with her election. Although Rob had been outwardly supportive of her mayoral run at the beginning, his enthusiasm had quickly waned. As it had turned out, he never thought anyone would take her campaign seriously.

She could still remember the wash of cold chills when she realized Rob had just been paying lip service and never expected her to be successful. He hadn't liked the amount of time JenniLynn was spending on the campaign and not catering to his needs. His selfish behavior was something she'd ignored for far too long.

When a series of events led to the discovery of a text chain between mayor elect Marty Moore and her own husband, and then a hidden box of paper ballots in a local warehouse, that had been the final straw. In police custody, Marty had spilled the beans on the entire scheme, but she'd known before that that she couldn't remain with Rob.

Not when it had started to feel like he'd grown weary of being a full-time family man. Rob had found reasons to spend more and more time away from home and used flimsy excuses that made her feel as if he viewed her as a fool. And maybe she was. JenniLynn had ignored her husband's distance at first because she didn't want it to be true. She still didn't know if there was another woman who'd shown him the attention he craved or if Rob had simply grown tired of her. Feeling unwanted was like a repeated punch to the gut.

A wave of depression threatened to engulf her, but as usual, she pushed it aside so she wouldn't fall apart. She had to be the strong one who picked up the pieces. Her three little girls were counting on her.

The whole election fiasco had been the final push she'd needed to file for divorce. Thank God getting sole custody of the girls hadn't been a problem. Rob now lived with his parents just out of town and rarely saw the girls. The whole experience had taught JenniLynn a lesson—she could only rely on herself, especially when it came to her kids.

Though doing such a high-pressure job without a partner was a lot harder than she'd counted on. Especially since none of her own family still lived in this area of Montana.

Lila came back into the room holding a framed family photo. "Mommy, is Mr. Grayson your boyfriend?"

She almost spit out her sparkling water and the bubbles stung her nose, but she managed to swallow and then cough before putting the bottle on the countertop. "No. He is not my boyfriend. I just met him today."

"I don't want a new daddy," Sasha whined and came over to fling her arms around her mommy's waist.

Her throat tightened. Apparently, her girls' thoughts were running along the same line as hers. They were all still adjusting to the hole in their family. JenniLynn picked up Sasha, went over to Lila and led her to the couch.

"Let's have a seat and talk." She gathered both girls into her arms. How had she been so blind and not seen how much it was still on their minds?

"Girls, there's no reason to worry or even talk about a new daddy. Hallie, honey, do you want to come talk to us about Daddy?"

Her two-year-old paused arranging her toys in a perfectly straight line long enough to glance at the ceiling and shake her head. Undisturbed by their conversation, she went right back to ignoring them.

JenniLynn's chest tightened. She hated to see how withdrawn her toddler had become since the divorce. Once upon a time, Hallie would've happily run over to join them. Her toddler just needed more time to adjust to the big changes in their family.

"You don't want a boyfriend?" Lila asked.

"No. I don't. Maybe someday, but for now it's just us four girls."

"Will you tell me when someday comes?" asked her oldest.

She was a bit taken aback. Talking to her children about dating was something she'd thought she'd only need to do once they were old enough to date themselves. "Yes, honey. We can talk about it if that time ever comes. But until then, we're going to do just fine. Don't you think so?"

"I think so," Lila agreed.

"Me, too," Sasha said loudly, not wanting to be left out, but Hallie still paid them no mind and straightened two of her dolls.

Lila put the framed photo face down on the couch cushion beside her. "Why did our daddy have to do something bad?"

JenniLynn kissed the top of her head and inhaled the green-apple scent of her shampoo. "I wish I could answer that, honey, but sometimes even moms don't have all the answers. Your daddy made some bad choices, and he has to face the consequences."

"And it's nothing we did, right?"

"Oh, my sweet Lila, it's definitely not anything you or your little sisters did."

"And nothing you did, either, Mommy?"

"That's right. Daddy made his own choices. But he loves you and he'll still come to visit." As rare as those visits had become, JenniLynn thought to herself.

"Can we have mash 'tatoes for dinner?" Sasha asked, changing the subject as small children are known to do.

"Yes. Mashed potatoes will go well with the baked chicken. Who wants to help me cook dinner?"

"I will." Lila jumped up and headed for the kitchen. "I want to use the mixer to mash the potatoes."

JenniLynn set the oven to preheat then opened the refrigerator and got out the chicken she'd marinated overnight in Italian dressing. "What did you do with Courtney after she picked you up?"

"We went to the library to read some books." Lila told her everything they did with their part-time babysitter after she picked them up from Little Cowpokes Daycare Center.

While she coated the tenders with seasoned breadcrumbs and put them on a baking sheet, Lila scrubbed and rinsed the potatoes. Her oldest filled a pot with water, and JenniLynn cut and dropped peeled potatoes into the water.

"Can I turn up the radio?" Sasha asked. "I like this song."

"Sure. I like it, too." JenniLynn sang along with them to the Tim McGraw song, and they danced around the kitchen island. The song was about cowboys, and it made her think of Grayson Abernathy. As if she'd taken a photo, his image was sharp in her mind, and the man looked really good in a Stetson.

As they cooked and ate, JenniLynn's thoughts continued to drift to Grayson, and every time they did, she reminded herself she'd just told her girls she didn't want a boyfriend. And it was true. She didn't. The ink on her divorce papers was barely dry, and she really hadn't begun to process the depth of Rob's betrayal. If she thought too deeply about it, she might fall apart.

She'd placed all her trust in the man she married and had a family with him, only to realize he wasn't worthy of her trust, and it had ended up hurting their children. If their own father couldn't be what they needed, how could she ever trust another man again?

She couldn't put her girls and herself through having someone else be in their lives who might eventually get tired of them. She would go it alone—which she now realized she'd already been doing when they were still married.

After the girls were bathed and bedtime stories had been read, everyone was finally tucked in. JenniLynn looked at the laptop and the stack of folders spread out on one side of her bed. The side where her husband used to sleep—before he blew up their life.

When she thought about Rob, it was definitely the hardcore cuss words running commentary through her brain. The father of her children had lost his right to her mild, made-up curses.

She plugged in her phone and set it on the nightstand. She had planned to grab a quick shower then look at the city budget to see where she could cut more unnecessary costs. There was work that needed doing, but all she really wanted was a nice hot bath before she crawled into bed to sleep. With a yawn, she made a decision. Just like cleaning out her purse, work could wait until tomorrow. If she wasn't rested, she was no good to anyone.

She undressed and put on her favorite red, silk robe before starting the water in the tub. Deciding to go full spa mode, she lit a couple of floral scented candles then went to the kitchen and poured half a glass of white wine. When she got back to her bedroom, her phone rang from her night-stand, and she glanced at the caller ID.

"It's Grayson!"

She sucked in a quick breath and pulled her robe together at the collar but then laughed at herself. It's not like he could see her. She hadn't even answered, but she should answer before his call went to voicemail or he hung up thinking that she didn't want to talk to him.

"Why am I overthinking this so much?" She snatched it up off her nightstand and answered. "Good evening."

"Hi, Mayor Garrett. It's Grayson Abernathy. Sorry to call so late."

"It's okay. I'm still awake." She usually liked being addressed by her title, but with Grayson it felt forced and odd. "Call me JenniLynn."

"Alright then, JenniLynn it is."

"What can I help you with this evening?" She was always helping someone, and the words came naturally to her.

"I have to go out of town earlier than expected and won't be able to make the meeting we set up."

"That's okay. I understand." JenniLynn swallowed unexpected disappointment and realized how much she'd been looking forward to seeing him again. "We can reschedule for another time."

"Can we possibly push the meeting up and meet tomorrow for lunch?" Grayson asked.

She had planned to eat a sandwich at her desk and mark a few things off her to-do list, but that's not what she said. "Where would you like to meet?"

"How about The Silver Spur Café at noon?"

"That works for me."

"Do I hear water running?"

"Oh! The water." She rushed into her bathroom and turned it off.

"Did I catch you in the bath?"

She could feel her skin flushing the same shade of scarlet as her robe. "Oh, no, I just finished filling the tub. I haven't…gotten in yet."

"Don't let me keep you from a nice relaxing soak. Maybe I should do the same."

The way his voice deepened made her shiver. "Maybe you should."

Of course, she immediately pictured the big, muscled cowboy in a deep tub with his black Stetson still on his head. She pressed her lips together to keep from giggling. "I'll see you at the café at noon."

"Goodnight, JenniLynn."

Butterflies, which she hadn't felt in quite some time, took flight in her belly. "Goodnight, Grayson."

She looked at the pale gray suit and white blouse hanging on the back of her closet door, all prepped to wear tomorrow with simple mid-height heels and pearl jewelry. But maybe she should wear something a little more colorful or fun tomorrow.

"What am I doing? This is not a date." It was a business meeting. She was not ready for a relationship of any kind. Romance was the last thing on her mind. Or at least it should be.

When JenniLynn arrived at The Silver Spur Cafe for her lunch meeting with Grayson, he was already sitting at a small table in one corner. His shoulders were so broad that he blocked the whole back of the wooden chair, and his pearl-snap button shirt was a shade of sapphire that magnified his blue eyes. The black Stetson she thought of last night was sitting on the table beside him. She'd seen him around town, but how had she never noticed how handsome he was?

He caught sight of her and waved.

She returned his smile and straightened her gray suit-coat, wishing she'd gone with her impulse and chosen a different outfit, but in her role as mayor it was important that she present a professional image. "I hope you haven't been waiting long."

"I just sat down," he said. "You have perfect timing."

She sat across from him and put her purse in the empty chair beside her. "I try to live by the motto, if you're not early, you're late."

"Good rule. Thanks for being so flexible and meeting today. I have to go out of town a few days earlier than expected to get my son."

"I didn't realize you are a dad."

"I am," Grayson said with a smile. "For the rest of the summer, I will have my nine-year-old son, Adam."

It was obvious he was excited about their upcoming visit, and that made her heart soften toward this tough cowboy. "That's wonderful." She was curious about the child's mother, but it was none of her business.

"I can't wait to see him."

She couldn't imagine not seeing her girls every day. "Is Adam the reason you had chewing gum in your hair?"

"Yep. He was riding on my shoulders, yawned and lost his gum and didn't tell me. I found it an hour later. But the fun we had that day was worth the hassle."

"I'm glad you'll be getting some time with him."

"He is very mature for his age, and I hope you won't mind if he tags along to some of our meetings or Job Corps events?"

"Of course not. He's welcome. My girls like to tag along

with me and see what I'm working on. I can't wait until Lila is old enough to file things for me. I always get behind on that task and end up with several piles on top of the conference table."

"I bet they are well-organized stacks."

She laughed. "I guess that depends on how you define *well organized*."

"I saw that you like to have your ink pens arranged a certain way."

"You noticed that?"

"I did."

"I do have a thing for pens and markers and colored pencils. You should see inside one of my desk drawers. They're arranged in cups by type and color. I like order and that's why the stacks I create drive me nuts."

"In your office before Brent and Barrett arrived, you were telling me about your grandmother's clock and the lessons she taught you."

She smiled at the memory of her fierce, sweet grandmother. "The clock was passed down to her from her own grandmother."

"Wow. It's got a lot of family history tied to it."

"It sure does. She always said that this clock reminded her to make time for a little fun in her day."

He asked about what other lessons she'd learned and shared a few of his own. Their natural rapport led to no lack of conversation. JenniLynn couldn't explain the connection with Grayson, but it made her feel…safe. Like she could breathe for just a little while and not have to be the only adult standing guard. She could relax for a moment and not have to be in fight-or-flight mode.

They ate and laughed and told stories until their waitress asked if they wanted dessert.

She placed her hands on her belly. "I can't eat another bite. But I would like a cup of coffee with cream."

"You've got it, Mayor Garrett. Anything for you, Mr. Abernathy?" the woman asked him as she tucked her hair behind her ear. Her voice changed to a slightly different tone when she talked to him.

"I'll have a cup as well," Grayson said and then looked up at the waitress with a smile. "Go ahead and bring a slice of apple pie, too, please."

The waitress blushed under his attention, and JenniLynn knew how she felt. The man was a charmer, but she was pretty sure he was also a big teddy bear.

He braced his folded arms on the table and leaned forward like he had a secret to tell. "I'm not sure how to tell you this, Mayor, but we forgot to talk about the Job Corps."

"Oh, you're right. Oops. I guess we better get down to business." From her purse, she pulled out her travel notebook along with a little plastic case that held her pens. She arranged them on the tabletop in front of her, and when she looked up at Grayson, he was grinning. "What has you smiling so big?"

"Nothing particular. Just in a good mood."

She found herself wishing it was because of her, but getting to see his son was likely the cause of his happiness.

They got down to business and discussed the "Job Corps Bootcamp" they'd like to run in a few weeks. They would be working with older teens and adults on the spectrum as well as business owners who wanted to be part of the program. They played with the idea of the bootcamp being one afternoon a week for a month, or a weekend. They decided to take a poll of people who might want to be involved before making a final decision.

"I think we have a good plan in place." He took his last

sip of coffee. "Do you want me to share it with Brent and Barrett?"

"That would be great. And don't forget to look for someone to work at my office."

"I won't forget."

She fiddled with her napkin, too curious not to ask. "Who is your son with right now?"

Grayson seemed to read her expression. "He's with my ex-wife. Luckily for me, she needs to go out of town for a business meeting, and I get him a few days early. Adam's mom and I have been divorced for five years. She is remarried now, and Adam has a good stepdad." He dipped his chin as if trying to hide his expression, but she caught a glimpse of pain in his blue eyes. "Sometimes things just don't work out the way you want."

JenniLynn knew that for sure. Rather than reaching across the table to take his hand and comfort him as she so wanted to do, she twisted her napkin into a tighter knot.

Chapter Three

"Hi, Dad!" Adam yelled and ran toward him.

"Hey, buddy." Grayson bent his knees and braced for the incoming flying hug. He caught his son and staggered slightly, surprised by the change in his weight. It was so good to have his boy in his arms again. Seeing him on a video chat just wasn't the same. He put Adam back on his feet. "I can't believe how much you've grown. You almost tackled me to the ground."

"Not you, Dad. You're too big and strong for me to tackle. But someday I'll be big enough, and I want to play football like you did in college."

"You do?"

"Mom said I can only play flag football right now." He rolled his eyes.

"We'll have to throw the football around. There's a perfect flat spot on the ranch." He loved that his son thought of him as strong. Adam was growing up way too fast, and he hated that he was missing so much of his life. He would have him with him all the time if he could.

"I can't wait to see your new ranch. Let's go right now." His little brown cowboy boots crunched the gravel as he spun on his heels and started for the truck.

"Hold up, buddy. I need to talk to your mother before we get on the road, and you don't have your suitcases."

"Oh, yeah." His little boy snapped his fingers and made an about-face. "I'm going to go get it and put all my stuff in your truck while you talk to Mom."

Grayson chuckled and walked toward his ex-wife, who was standing near the front door smiling at their son. At the age of thirty, Grayson had married Rebecca when she discovered she was pregnant. They hadn't known each other for very long, but Adam was born six months later. They had tried to make their marriage work for the sake of their child, but ultimately, they realized they were better off as friends. They got an amicable divorce when Adam was four and had shared custody ever since.

But there were days he wished he'd fought harder to remain a family. He hated coming home to a house that was empty and quiet. He'd even started putting the television on a timer so it was on when he came inside in the evenings.

"Hi, Rebecca." He hugged her and then waved to her husband John, who was coming out of the garage with two suitcases and headed for Grayson's new silver truck.

"Good to see you, Grayson. Adam is so excited about his time with you. I sure am going to miss him, but I'm glad you two will get some time together."

"I've really been looking forward to it. Have you heard anything about the promotion you want?"

She shook her head. "Not yet. Hopefully it won't be much longer, and I'll know what options I have to work with."

Adam ran up and wrapped his arms around his mother's waist. "I love you, Mom."

Grayson stepped away to give them a few minutes to say goodbye. He knew all too well what it was like to miss their son. It sucked.

Once they were on the way back to Tenacity and playing their favorite road-trip soundtrack, Adam wanted to hear all about the ranch. He couldn't wait to see the new Montana spread.

"There is a big sturdy barn, well-built stables, a great pond and, of course, the river."

"Are there trees to climb?"

"Tons of them. I've even picked out a few that might be good for a treehouse."

"Oh, cool. I've always wanted a treehouse."

Grayson turned on the wipers when a light rain began to fall. "This summer, I'm going to be working on a program to help people on the autism spectrum find jobs. We're going to call it Tenacity Job Corps, and we're going to have a bootcamp."

"To teach them how to do pushups and stuff?"

He couldn't hold back the grin. "Not exactly. More about teaching people how they can help people like your cousin Oscar be successful."

"Ooh! Can I help you?"

"I was hoping you would want to. I would love your help."

"I can't wait, Dad. I'm going to help you as much as I can."

Adam was such a happy kid, and Grayson was thankful Rebecca had done such a great job with him. After a couple of hours, Adam fell asleep with his head leaning against the window, and although Grayson loved hearing his son's happy chatter, it gave him time to admire his little boy. In sleep, he looked younger. So innocent and defenseless. He had always been small for his age, but he'd had a growth spurt since Grayson had last seen him in person.

He shook his head and adjusted the air conditioner. It was time to stop whining about what he'd missed out on.

He couldn't go backward. They had the rest of the summer together, and now that his new ranch was a little closer to where Adam lived with his mother, he was going to talk to Rebecca about adding more visits with him throughout the year.

When a slow country love song came on the radio, Grayson's thoughts shifted to JenniLynn, and it made his blood heat. Dancing with her was a very appealing idea, but ever since his failed marriage, he'd become very careful about who he dated, and dating while Adam was with him was not an option.

He shook his head. Daydreaming about JenniLynn was fun, but because of her situation combined with his, this line of thinking was a bad idea.

How hard it must be for her raising three girls all on her own. She acted like it was no big deal, but he knew better.

When they arrived in Tenacity around dinnertime that night, they stopped to eat at Castillo's Mexican Restaurant. He was way too tired to go home and cook, and he knew his son would love the food here. Right inside the door, he spotted JenniLynn and her three girls, as if his recent thoughts had conjured them. They sat in a booth with JenniLynn on one side with Hallie in a booster and Sasha near the wall. Lila sat alone on the other side.

"Look, Mommy. It's Mr. Grayson," Sasha said. She once again had two braids and a mischievous smile that made her eyes squint.

JenniLynn put down her menu and pulled off a pair of pink reading glasses. "Hi. It's nice to see you again."

"You, too. Hello, ladies," he said to her girls. "This is my son, Adam. Adam, this is Mayor JenniLynn Garrett," he said and grinned when she rolled her eyes at him about his use of her official title.

"Hello, Adam. These are my girls, Lila, Sasha and Hallie."

At the sound of her name, the toddler leaned in her booster seat to hide her face in the crook of her mother's arm.

"Would you two like to join us? We can pull up a chair on the end of our booth, so you don't have to wait for a table."

Grayson started to decline, but Adam slid onto the bench seat beside Lila.

"I'm starved," Adam said.

Lila pushed the basket of tortilla chips his way. "These are really yummy, but the salsa is hot. So be careful."

"Thanks." He had crammed two chips into his mouth before Grayson could even say they'd accept JenniLynn's offer.

An employee who'd heard their exchange brought over a chair. JenniLynn smiled shyly at Grayson as he sat, their knees brushing and sending a tingle along his skin. It was a little dim in the cozy restaurant, but he could clearly see the rosy glow on the lovely mayor's cheeks.

The restaurant owner, Yolanda Castillo, came over with two glasses of ice water and a wide smile. "What can I get for you boys?"

"We will have the beef fajitas for two, please."

"Can we get chips and queso, too, please, Dad?"

"Absolutely. Sounds great, buddy."

"Good choices," Yolanda said. "I just put the girls' order in so everything should be out around the same time."

"Thanks, Yolanda," he said and took a long sip of cold water.

"Did you just move here?" Lila asked Adam.

"I'm visiting my dad for the rest of the summer. He has a new ranch called Ambling Hills."

"We live on a ranch, too," her seven-year-old said. "It's called Coyote Creek Ranch."

"Want to come fishing on our ranch?" Adam asked the girls. "My dad got new fishing poles."

Lila wrinkled her nose. "I've never touched a live fish."

"I'm afraid that's my fault," JenniLynn said. "I've never taken them fishing."

Adam's jaw dropped open. "Never?"

Both adults bit back a chuckle.

"Even though I grew up in the country, I don't know how to fish," JenniLynn admitted.

"I can teach you," Grayson said. The words tumbled out in a natural flow, but now that the offer was out there, he really hoped she'd take him up on it. "All four of you."

"I wanna catch a fishy," Sasha said as she climbed onto her knees to reach the basket of chips and drag it her way.

"Well then." JenniLynn worried her lip as if she was about to take a big risk. "It looks like the Garrett girls are going to learn how to fish." Hallie looked up at her mother with a fearful expression, and she put her arm around her tiny daughter and kissed her forehead. "It will be fun, sweet girl."

Grayson still hadn't heard the toddler make a single sound, and he couldn't help but wonder if it had something to do with her father's scandal and dramatic exit from their lives. It made a sudden anger build within him. How could a father do what Rob Garrett had done to his own wife and children? Grayson would give anything to have a big family, and this stupid man hadn't appreciated or valued them enough to protect them.

Sasha burped, and the kids' laughter pulled him back to the current moment. It was a good reminder that he needed to grab every second of fun with his son.

"Sasha, what do you say now?" JenniLynn asked her with a pointed stare.

"Thank you." The little girl put her hand over her mouth and giggled. "I mean, excuse me."

"We've been working on remembering our manners," Lila explained to Adam. "Sometimes she gets them confused."

"I think she's funny," he said, and that made Sasha smile even bigger.

He and JenniLynn shared a smile of their own. He was suddenly really glad they'd run into the Garrett girls. Now, Adam already had friends in town, and Grayson got the pleasure of the lovely mayor's company. And this close, she smelled really good. Like peaches and sunshine.

Even though the timing was all wrong for dating, there was no rule against enjoying their time together when the occasion arose.

The children laughed about something else, and a plan formed in his mind. If their kids were friends, he might see a bit more of her.

Before he even saw it, Grayson caught the savory scent of onions and peppers and heard the sizzle of his beef fajitas on a cast iron platter. His mouth began to water.

"Wow. Look at that!" Adam said. "Dad, is that our fajitas?"

"I believe it is. Looks good, doesn't it?"

"It's smoking. Is it gonna catch fire?" Sasha was up on her knees again.

"Sit down flat on your bottom," JenniLynn said. "It's not going to catch on fire, but it is very hot, so no touching the platter."

"Okay, Mommy."

"There is a reason I put her on the inside of the booth,"

she whispered to him. "Otherwise, she'd be jumping up to talk to people at other tables."

He chuckled and glanced around at the other diners. Many of them were looking their way, some trying to hide it and others more openly gawking. They no doubt wanted to know how this new guy had scored a dinner invitation with their mayor.

Plates were passed out, and they were both busy assisting children with their food, but they snuck in a few smiles.

"I barely remember what it's like to eat my food while it's still hot," she said to him with a chuckle and picked up her own fork.

"That's the mark of a good parent." Grayson added a healthy dose of hot sauce to his food.

"I like that way of thinking." She forked in a bite and then closed her eyes as she chewed with a little sigh.

He bit his cheek to keep from chuckling. He found her enjoyment of her food both funny and sexy.

Throughout the meal, there was only one spilled drink—laughably, his fault—and one squabble between sisters.

A glob of cheese flew off the spoon Sasha was flinging around across from them and landed splat on the pocket of Grayson's shirt.

"Oh, fudgesicle," JenniLynn said and put her hands momentarily over her eyes.

This wasn't the first time he'd heard her creative cursing, and he pressed his lips together to keep from laughing.

"Sorry," the little girl said quickly and looked worried until he grinned.

Grayson scraped the dip from his shirt and licked the cheese off his finger. "Thanks for sharing."

Sasha giggled, and the other kids joined in.

"Fudgesicle?" he asked quietly enough for only Jenni-Lynn to hear.

Her soft laugh was a musical sound. "I promised myself I wouldn't use cuss words around my girls, so I came up with a few of my own."

"I can't wait to hear what other gems you have in your repertoire."

A pretty pink blush feathered across her high cheekbones, and he realized how his words might have sounded. Like he was looking forward to getting to know her. Did she like the idea of spending more time together? Because he sure did.

"There's a likely chance that learning to fish will elicit a couple of them," she said.

He really hoped so, because he found her creative cursing kind of adorable.

An elderly man he had never seen before patted Grayson on the shoulder on his way by their table. "Lovely group of youngsters. You're a lucky man."

"Thank you," he said as an auto response and noticed JenniLynn biting her lip as if she was trying hard to hide her expression. Was it a smile, or was it a grimace?

"Why are you lucky?" Sasha asked him.

"Because I get to have dinner with all of you."

"Oh. Okay." That explanation seemed to satisfy the curious four-year-old, and she went back to eating her cheese enchiladas.

The man's comment didn't leave him so easily. The words kept repeating in his head like a scratched record.

Lovely group of youngsters. You're a lucky man.

Once upon a time, he assumed he would have a big family of his own by now. Not living alone and only seeing his kid in the summer and on holidays and assigned weekends. His ex was good about letting him see Adam other times, too, but it was still hard. Still not enough to fill the emptiness.

When the checks came, they each paid their own bill, and all walked out onto the sidewalk together. "I'll give you a call about fishing at my place," he said.

"Sounds good." JenniLynn motioned for Lila to take Sasha's hand. "I'll look at our schedule when I get home."

Grayson smiled at the toddler on JenniLynn's hip. "I'll see you later, Hallie."

Hallie tilted her head against her mommy's chest, and with her eyes once again cast at his feet, a brief smile lifted one corner of her mouth. It was progress. They all said their goodbyes and walked in opposite directions to their cars.

"Dad, is that lady your girlfriend?" Adam asked the second they walked away.

"No, son. I don't have a girlfriend."

"She likes to smile at you."

That news brought his own happy expression. Grayson had been sneaking glances as she sat right beside him. Had she been doing the same? "Does she?"

"Yep. She does. If you married her, like mom got married again…" Adam scratched his head and then looked up at him with an unreadable expression. "That would be a lot of sisters."

His son's innocent words made him momentarily speechless. The images popping into his mind were ones that made him hopeful. "It sure would be."

He stopped himself before asking if Adam wanted brothers or sisters. Being one of six children, Grayson often felt guilty that his son was growing up an only child.

His family was always asking him why he was still single—a good-looking guy with wads of money—but after a rushed and then failed marriage, he was wary of getting involved again. He never wanted to go through another divorce. He had loved Adam's mother, but being *in love* was different. The next time he committed to someone, he needed to be 100 percent sure that marriage was for the right reasons. Namely, a deep shared love. The kind that made you dream about growing old and gray together with matching rockers on a front porch and grandchildren playing in the front yard.

Although he felt ready to take dating more seriously, the timing was wrong. He was just settling into his new community and devoting this time to Adam. Thinking about hooking up with his new town's mayor was best put aside. At least for now.

Chapter Four

JenniLynn stood in front of her bathroom mirror in her third outfit change of the morning. It wasn't like she was some city girl who didn't know what was appropriate to wear fishing. She'd grown up on a ranch, but for some reason, choosing what to wear while fishing with a man she found attractive was presenting a challenge. It also made her feel a bit like a giggly teenager.

The dark, wide-leg jeans had felt too dressy, and none of her shorts fit right, so her comfy worn-in jeans would have to do. She turned from side to side to inspect her reflection and was pleased with the fit. An emerald-green cotton top gave her outfit a casual without being sloppy vibe.

She went out into the living room where the girls were watching a morning cartoon. The sweet sight made her smile. Her oldest was in the middle with her arms around her two younger sisters. Three little blonde heads huddled together. She was so blessed to have them in her life.

"Girls, your clothes are laid out on your beds. We are leaving in thirty minutes."

"Okay, Mommy," Lila said. "I already gathered the eggs while you were putting on your makeup."

"Thank you, sweetie. You are such a big help." Jenni-Lynn smiled to herself on the way into the kitchen to prepare the picnic lunch she'd offered to bring. She packed up cold cuts, cheeses, several kinds of bread, chips, fruit and, of course, her signature brown butter pecan cookies. She'd made friends with a pastry chef and been given the recipe at a small-town bakery on a trip to the Texas Hill Country, where they'd stayed in the quaint town of Oak Hollow.

Once everyone had on their matching pink rubber boots, they loaded up into their SUV. It was a short drive from Coyote Creek, the family ranch she'd grown up on, to Ambling Hills.

"Mommy, can we put on the disco songs?" Lila requested.

"Sure." She pulled it up on her phone, and their favorite Bee Gees' album started playing before she backed out of the garage.

Lila and Sasha sang along to "Staying Alive," their sweet voices blending rather nicely. In the rearview mirror, she caught glimpses of Hallie clapping and kicking her feet in time with the beat.

After four songs, she slowed, turned onto a driveway and stopped at an iron gate. An arch above it had scrollwork letters that read *Ambling Hills*. She rolled down her window to enter the four-digit code Grayson had given her.

"What's that say?" Sasha asked from the back seat.

"It says, Ambling Hills." The gate swung wide, and she drove farther along the tree-lined driveway. Ponderosa pines fluffed full and Douglas fir trees stood tall and straight, like a welcoming parade of majestic old soldiers.

"Am bing hills. Am bing," Sasha repeated.

"No," Lila said to her little sister. "Am-bling. Bling. Like the way we call Mommy's sparkly purse her bling."

Her four-year-old gasped with delight. "Do they have glitter on their house? Is this a sparkly ranch?"

JenniLynn chuckled at her middle child. "I don't think

it will be very sparkly, sweetheart." She couldn't imagine Grayson decorating his home with anything that fit that feminine-leaning description. He was more…

She drummed her fingers on the steering wheel as she considered it. She wasn't sure how to describe this cowboy. Not yet. Maybe today would give her a fuller picture of her new neighbor. A better idea of how far, or not, she should take their growing friendship.

When they pulled up to Grayson's, he and Adam were on the front porch of his log cabin–style house. No bling in sight. Other than the smile on the cowboy's face that created sparks in her belly.

"There's that man and little boy," Sasha exclaimed excitedly.

"Their names are Mr. Grayson and Adam," Lila told her little sister.

They all piled out, but Hallie clung to her and did not want to be put down after JenniLynn unbuckled and got her out of her car seat. "Ready for some fun?"

"Puppy?" Hallie said.

"I don't see any puppies."

Lila, Sasha and Adam had no trouble greeting one another and were already talking about who would catch the biggest fish.

Grayson smiled and waved, making JenniLynn's stomach perform a flip. From his black Stetson to his cowboy boots, he was a head turner. Even though his jeans were old and well worn in and his maroon pearl-snap shirt was faded from many washes, there was nothing sloppy about this cowboy.

Sasha stared at the house with her hands on her hips and her feet braced wide. "You were right, Mommy. It's not a sparkly house."

Grayson followed the little girl's gaze. "Was I supposed to put up something sparkly?"

"I just thought maybe it would be…" Sasha sighed. "But boys don't like bling."

Grayson turned an amused and quizzical expression JenniLynn's way.

"It's a long story," she said.

"Dad, can I show them my room and my star maker?"

"If it's okay with their mom," he replied.

"It's fine with me." She put Hallic on her feet, and she ran over to be with her sisters and Adam as they went inside the house.

They followed the kids through the front door. "We decorated Adam's bedroom in a space theme, and he just got a machine that projects the constellations onto the ceiling. I guess he wants to show it off."

"How fun." The savory scent of bacon hung in the air, giving her a pretty good clue as to what they'd had for breakfast. She looked around the sparsely appointed living room. It was neat and tidy. Rustic with what looked like new furniture that was comfortable and easily lived in. A fireplace made of smooth river stones anchored the room, and a bank of large windows showcased the amazing Montana view. "This is a lovely house. Cozy but spacious at the same time."

"It's bigger than I needed, but I like it."

There was a sturdy wooden bookcase along one wall that held trophies, books, framed photos and three old clocks. "Do you like clocks, too?"

"I do. That's why I was interested in yours."

"I was right!" Sasha's voice echoed through the house.

He chuckled, but JenniLynn sighed and automatically went toward the sound of excitement to see why her daughter was shouting.

"What are you right about?" she asked from the doorway of the darkened room.

Sasha pointed at the ceiling where lights flickered and almost seemed to dance over the surface. "Sparkles."

"They're not sparkles," Adam insisted. "They're stars."

"I think I need to hear this long story about sparkles," Grayson said in a low tone.

Even Hallie seemed content to stretch out on the floor and stare up at the twinkling lights, so JenniLynn left them to play. "Let's go sit where it's a little quieter, and I'll fill you in on sparkle and bling."

"A subject I never thought I'd want to know about, but I do. Would you like a cup of coffee before we head down to the river?"

"I think I would." In his sunny kitchen, she took a seat at a round table in his breakfast nook and started her story. He was very entertained as she filled him in on the funny confusion over his ranch's name.

"I can't say I ever would have figured out that line of thinking, but I admire it." He stared into his coffee and fiddled with a chip on the rim of his mug. "Aren't the minds of little kids amazing? We should slow down more often and pay attention to what they have to tell us about the world."

She was momentarily speechless. It was such an insightful statement that it had caught her off guard. Those thoughtful words never would have come out of Rob's mouth. Paying attention wasn't one of his strong suits. He'd rarely truly listened to her, much less the kids.

But Grayson was...different.

"You are so right about listening to kids," she said, a bit delayed. "You're very observant, aren't you?"

"I try to be." His smile was proud, as if she'd given him a big compliment.

She checked on the kids once, but while they played happily in Adam's room, the two of them continued talking and laughing at the kitchen table. It was nice to sit across the table with an adult, sipping morning coffee and sneaking some of the cookies she'd brought. She'd yet to discover one thing about him that hinted at why he was divorced.

So she asked him. Outright.

She gasped the second the words left her lips. "I'm so sorry. I can't believe I said that out loud."

Ugh! What is wrong with me? She wanted to hide under the table.

Grayson's grin turned into a full smile. "Don't worry about it. But I am sad I didn't get to hear another one of your creative curses."

"I promise to dazzle you with one later."

"To answer your question about my divorce…"

"Oh, my gosh. You don't have to." Her cheeks flamed. "That was so rude of me to even ask."

"I figure since I know some things about your rather public divorce, it's only fair."

"I cringe at what you've heard. People do like to talk, and facts often change with each retelling."

"You can set the record straight if you ever want to talk about it."

Now he was offering to listen to her story? "I appreciate the offer. You go first."

"Rebecca and I hadn't been dating long when she got pregnant. We got married, and we really tried to make it work, but ultimately, we're better as friends."

"So, it was an amicable divorce?"

"It was."

"I'm glad, because I know the alternative."

The sympathy in his expression was obvious. "I hate that for you."

She twirled a lock of hair around her finger as she looked into her mug. "With every challenge comes a lesson. It has taught me a few things. I'm learning how to count on myself, and I'm discovering my own strength. It's rather empowering to be in charge."

"You are definitely a woman in charge."

"Oh, I didn't mean being the mayor gives me power." The last thing she wanted to be seen as was power hungry.

"I know. I didn't mean that, either. You are kicking butt as a mom."

She returned his smile. "Thanks for noticing. My goal is not to rush myself or my situation. I'm giving myself plenty of time to heal and adjust to my new phase of life."

"Wise move." He slid his hand across the table as if he'd take hers.

JenniLynn's breath caught, unsure what she wanted to happen next.

"Mommy! Hallie needs to go to the bathroom!" her oldest daughter yelled from the other room.

She took her last sip of coffee, put down her mug and braced her hands flat on the table. "Well, I guess our coffee—" She caught herself just before saying coffee "date." "Our break is over," she said instead.

"Looks that way."

After everyone had made a trip to the bathroom, they loaded up into the back of Grayson's truck, and he slowly drove out to the river that ran through his ranch.

On a flat spot under a large tree near the water, she spread out a thickly quilted picnic blanket that she'd bought years ago for just such an occasion. Finally using it fit right into her plan to make positive changes in her life. She weighed down the canvas material with the picnic basket and her backpack of other items they might need throughout the day.

Grayson started the two older girls out with kids' fishing poles and explained how the pole was called a rod and the part that held the spool of fishing line was called the reel. Instead of real hooks for now, there was only a small rubber fish on the end of the line that gave it enough weight to practice casting. Hallie even wanted a turn.

Adam helped the girls while Grayson got the adult-sized rods and reels ready. He opened a tackle box, and JenniLynn peered inside at the array of colorful choices, all sorted neatly in little compartments. "So, no real worms or bugs to put on a hook?"

"No." He turned a sly grin her way. The kind of grin that reminded her of one she might get from Sasha. "But if you want a worm, I'm sure we can dig up a few."

"Oh, no. I'm quite glad that we're not using anything that is alive." An artificial fly was a much more humane method in her opinion.

"Let me know if you change your mind."

"Don't hold your breath." She added the characteristic "playful" to her mental list of things she was discovering about him.

He took a few minutes demonstrating how to cast.

"I think I've got it. I'm ready to try." JenniLynn flicked the tip of her rod back but released the line too soon and ended up catching her hook in the tree behind her.

"Wrong way, Mommy," Sasha yelled helpfully.

She tried to yank it free. "Oh, spadoodle."

Grayson burst into laughter, and she wasn't sure if his amusement was because of her pitiful fishing skills or inventive choice of words, but she couldn't resist laughing right along with him and the kids.

"That's the best one yet. Spadoodle," he said between laughs.

"Hopefully that will make up for my rude personal question in your kitchen."

"Totally does. Let me help you."

"So…how did you choose the name of your ranch?" she asked him while he untangled her line.

"My family's ranch is Ambling A, so me choosing Ambling Hills is a nod to that heritage."

"I love that. Do you come from a big family?"

"Yes. I'm one of six children. I have two sisters and three brothers." He told her a few funny childhood memories and his hope that some of his siblings would visit them soon.

"I hope my girls will someday smile about their childhood memories like you do," JenniLynn said when he was done.

"I'm sure they will. Sasha is going to be so disappointed with the dull explanation of my ranch's name, won't she?"

"Maybe you can make up a more theatrical version for her," she suggested.

"I'll see what I can come up with."

His crooked grin made her think he would actually do it, and she couldn't wait to see what he came up with.

Grayson spent the majority of his time going from child to child and helping with one thing or another. He also made sure everyone got to reel in a fish.

Sasha held her small fish with both hands and lifted it to eye level. "Thanks for letting me catch you. Bye-bye." She puckered her lips.

"No, ma'am!" JenniLynn stuck her hand between the animal and her child's mouth. "You cannot kiss that fish."

The little girl shrugged, squatted and gently put it into the water and watched it swim away.

Adam was giggling, but Lila looked horrified that her little sister would even consider such a disgusting thing. Grayson appeared well entertained as he smiled to himself and cast his line back out into the rippling water.

JenniLynn internally sighed and admired his athletic body as he moved. Why did he have to be so good with her girls? It made it ten times harder to find reasons to stay away from him. Jumping into anything with a man so soon after her divorce was ridiculous. An epically bad idea. Her kids had already been hurt because she'd trusted the wrong person. Her heart began to pound uncomfortably.

I'm not ready. She pressed a hand flat against her rib cage, trying to calm her racing heart. *I can't rush myself.*

With a triumphant whoop, Grayson reeled in a big fish and then turned to show it off to the kids. They all cheered, and her tension began to melt away.

She thought about their lunch meeting at the Silver Spur Café and their coffee date in his kitchen. Talking to him was fun. She might not be ready for a romance, but a friend…

I could use a friend.

Hallie hooked an arm around JenniLynn's leg and rested her head against her thigh. "Hello, sweet girl. Are you hungry or tired?"

"Eat, Mommy." Her sweet little voice was always such a joy to hear.

"I'm ready to eat, too. Who's hungry?" she called out to the others. A chorus of agreements blended in with the music of rushing water and chirping birds.

The first thing she got out was a bottle of sanitizer and a packet of wet wipes for their fishy hands. She started passing out the wipes and then opened a small trash bag. "Make sure to get between your fingers."

"Dad, how come you don't bring hand cleaning stuff when it's just us fishing?"

"Well…" He tossed his dirty wipe into the designated bag. "I'm a rancher—I'm used to getting my hands dirty."

"Boys have cooties," Sasha said in a singsong voice and giggled.

"So do girls," Adam said, and lifted both of her braids out to the side.

"Right now, you all have cooties," JenniLynn told all of them. "Get busy with the hand cleaning."

Grayson patted his son's back. "Sit still so you don't spill anything."

"I have an idea," she said. "Whoever can be the best frozen statue gets to put in their sandwich order first."

All the kids struck a pose, and Grayson encouraged them while JenniLynn spread everything out. "Okay, who will it be?" she asked.

"And the winner is…" He performed a drumroll. "Hallie."

Her sweet toddler clapped for herself, and everyone joined the celebration. JenniLynn sprinkled some goldfish-shaped crackers onto a paper plate, and Hallie started lining them up while she made her daughter a half of a sandwich with ham and cheese.

"I've discovered this short-order cook–style picnic is easier than trying to take things off a sandwich after the fact. Especially with something like pickles," she told Grayson.

"Smart. I'll work on Adam's. Could you hand me a plate?" Their fingers brushed and they both paused. There was a second of sizzle, as if it had triggered a hidden switch.

Lila yelped as she flicked a bug off her leg, and their moment ended.

Was she just imagining these little moments, or was there a real connection between her and Grayson?

While they ate their lunch, a couple of chipmunks chattered in the tree beside them and a brave little bird hopped over to steal some crumbs from their blanket. JenniLynn soaked up every minute of joy, pushed aside her worries and counted her blessings.

Sunlight cut through the tree branches and glinted off the girls' shiny blond hair. A light breeze lifted Lila's long hair, so much like her own. It made her think of being seven years old and believing the world would give her any opportunity she wanted to go after. Wispy curls escaped Sasha's braids and formed around her face, fluttering in the warm afternoon breeze, and Hallie's curls made her look like a little angel.

Once the meal was done, the kids flew a red-and-yellow kite and blew bubbles while she and Grayson remained on the picnic blanket.

JenniLynn gathered the last of the lunch trash and stuffed it into a plastic bag. She shielded her eyes and looked toward the eastern fence line. "Did you know that part of your ranch and mine almost connect?"

His gaze followed the direction she pointed. "Really? I didn't know that."

"There's only a small piece of property between them. That strip of land belongs to Mr. Smith."

"I've met him. He seems like a nice man."

"He's wonderful, and he has always been a great neighbor."

"I've seen his cattle grazing in that pasture. It's a fine herd."

She grinned, feeling rather proud. "Those are *my* cattle. He lets me graze my herd on his land because he only has twenty head left."

He rolled to his side and propped his head up on one hand. "Is that right? Impressive. How do you do it all?"

"With help. Mr. Smith has been my ranch manager ever since…" She hesitated. Saying too much about her messy divorce would lead her back down some painful pathways. Those were memories she didn't feel like getting into on such a beautiful July afternoon.

"Since you've been a single mom running a whole town?" he asked while she tried to decide what to say.

"Exactly. But Mr. Smith is getting older and recently informed me that he won't be able to do it for much longer. Even though I do pay him, I think he has only been doing it as a favor to me. He saw me struggling after I became mayor."

"That makes me like him even more." Grayson twirled a leaf between his long fingers. "Are you searching for a new foreman?"

She sighed and then leaned back on her elbows and crossed her outstretched legs at the ankles. "It's on my list of things to do, but it keeps getting pushed aside for more pressing matters. If I'm not careful, I'll wait too long and end up adding another job to my schedule. Especially since Mr. Smith has been talking about selling his small farm and moving closer to his children."

Grayson took off his hat and put it onto the blanket beside him then brushed his fingers through his short hair. "I'm sure we can find someone to help you out."

His use of the word *we* made her stomach flutter.

He's just being neighborly. He didn't mean it like that.

There was no "we" here.

"Are you going to buy his farm if he sells?" he asked.

She shook her head. "No. I don't need more on my plate than I already have."

"It's good that you know when to say no to something."

"Well, that's debatable."

"Have you always lived on Coyote Creek Ranch?"

"Most of my life. I grew up there. My parents used to run it, but they've moved to a warmer climate, and we took over for them."

"Mommy," Lila yelled and waved to them. "Come see what Adam found."

Hallie squealed, pulled away from her big sister and ran toward JenniLynn, her tiny pink boots flapping against her little legs.

JenniLynn got up and scooped her youngest into her arms. "What did he find, sweetie?"

Her big blue eyes were wide as she clasped her mommy's cheeks. "Wizard."

"A lizard? Oh, my goodness. Was it big?"

Hallie nodded and then yawned before resting her head on her shoulder.

"I'll go see what they have," Grayson said.

"Thank you. This one is not a fan of reptiles." She cuddled her sleepy toddler and watched Grayson with the other three kids. He was good with them. He knew how to be just silly enough to entertain them, but at the same time, he knew when to be the adult whenever it was called for. At least that was the impression she got so far.

Once the lizard scampered away, she and Hallie joined the others.

"Take our picture, Mommy." Lila put an arm around her little sister's shoulders but stopped herself before putting her other arm around Adam.

Hallie wiggled on her hip, and she put her down. "Get in the photo with your sisters and Adam. Everyone, strike a funny pose."

An impromptu photo session broke out as she and Grayson took photos of the kids and of each other. She made sure to get a few of Grayson and Adam together so he would have a visual reminder of his time with his son.

She scrolled through some of the fun images she'd just captured. "I got a great shot of you and Adam. I'll send it to you."

"Thanks. I'll send you some, too."

Hallie began to fuss and show all the signs that she was overtired. "I'm sorry to say that afternoon naptime is calling."

"Understandable. I'll start loading the truck." He moved quickly to gather everything.

Once the girls were buckled into their seats in her SUV, she stood at her open driver's-side door and smiled at Grayson. "I know your time with your son is precious. Thank you for including us in some of it."

"Adam had a blast. And so did I." He stepped closer and shifted his cowboy hat farther back on his head, giving her a better view of his ruggedly handsome face. It was almost as if he was…preparing to kiss her.

Time slowed as the air around them seemed to vibrate. His blue eyes twinkled with mischief.

"Mommy! Let's go, please," Sasha said.

He stepped back and chuckled. "At least she said please."

"Progress. Bye, Grayson."

"Goodbye, Mayor Jenni."

She got in, closed the door and started the car. Everyone waved as they drove away. JenniLynn couldn't help but wonder, if they'd been alone in that moment, would he have leaned in to kiss her? She suddenly knew one way to describe her hot rancher neighbor.

Adorably irresistible.

But resisting his charms was exactly what she had to do.

Chapter Five

Grayson watched the Garrett girls drive away and then went up onto the porch where Adam was using a bright yellow watering can to water the flowers they'd added to the window boxes. The colorful plants made the house look a little more like a home, but having his son with him was by far the best transformation.

Since his divorce, he'd been okay with being a bachelor until the right one came along, because the next time he had to get it right. But having JenniLynn and her girls here was a teasing taste of what it would be like to have a big family of his own. Maybe it was time to seriously consider putting himself out there and dating, once Adam was back in school.

He certainly wasn't getting any younger. With a deep sigh, he sat in one of his new Adirondack chairs.

Mayor JenniLynn Garrett was just getting her feet back under her after an emotional divorce and, judging by a few comments she'd made, not in a place to start a new relationship. Not to mention, she was loved by pretty much everyone in town and messing things up with her after everything she'd been through would be a disaster. The residents of Tenacity would most likely run him out of town. And if he hurt her, he would deserve it.

There was also the chance that he would be the one who

got hurt when he fell for a woman who couldn't return his feelings. A gust of wind blew under the porch roof, and he took off his hat and put it on the table beside him. The wind blew through his short hair and cooled his skin.

"Dad, there's a butterfly on the flowers."

"That's cool. What else do you see?" He had always encouraged his son to be observant of nature and his surroundings in general. It was an important skill for everyone, especially farmers and ranchers who made their living off the land. Grayson believed that developing good observational skills led to curiosity and improved critical thinking.

This was one of the things he enjoyed most about his relationship with his neurodivergent clients. They almost always had a perspective or an observation he would never have made on his own. His goal was to offer support and strategies to enhance their well-being.

"Hey, there's a ladybug and some roly-polies in the dirt."

He watched Adam inspect the area and then put away the watering can and head his way. His little boy slid back into the other chair, the depth and angle of the seat lifting his feet enough that only the heels of his cowboy boots touched the porch boards.

"Did you have fun today, buddy?"

"Yep. Sometimes girls aren't so bad." He stretched an arm above his head to touch the wind chime that Grayson's cousin had given him as a housewarming gift.

He grinned at his nine-year-old. "I agree. Girls can be a lot of fun."

"Sasha is funny, and Lila likes the same book series I do. I guess that's what it would be like to have lots of sisters."

"Do you wish you had brothers and sisters?" He had worried about this before and felt guilty about Adam being an only child.

"Sometimes. Dad, do you want more kids?"

The question surprised him, and he wasn't sure how to answer. But honesty was always the best option. "I wouldn't mind having a few more kids."

"Is it because I'm with mom a lot?"

He leaned forward and put his hand on Adam's knee. "Hey, listen to me and know this. Even if I never have any more kids, you are all I'll ever need. You are enough for me, and I'm so proud of you."

"But if God wants you to have more kids…then it's okay with you?"

Grayson smiled at his son. "I couldn't have said it better myself."

"Can we have pizza for dinner and watch a movie?" Adam asked, apparently ready to move on to the next topic.

"You bet. Why don't we go get the rest of the chores done first and then we can relax."

"What do we have to do?"

"I need to bring in the horses from the pasture to the stable, check a few of the mama cows and put out some molasses blocks. Can you help me?"

He jumped to his feet. "I'll be the best helper ever. Let's go."

Happy to see his eagerness, Grayson pushed himself up and put on his hat. "You're hired, cowboy."

With the television droning in the background late that night, Grayson was seconds away from dozing off on the couch when his phone rang. Jerking upright, he groaned and looked at the caller ID, but his annoyance turned into a smile when he saw the photograph he'd programmed for JenniLynn's number. Four blonde beauties all smiling.

He answered with a smile. "Hello, Mayor."

The little-girl giggle on the other end of the phone line was definitely not JenniLynn's. "I'm Sasha. Not the mayor."

His confusion quickly shifted into amusement. "Hello, Sasha. Does your mom know you're using her phone?"

"No. She's singing in a bubble bath and thinks I'm in bed."

He chuckled again. At least this mischievous little girl was an honest rascal. He suddenly wished Sasha was close enough to her mother for him to hear JenniLynn singing. "Did you call me all by yourself?"

"Yep. I'm a big girl."

He turned off the television. "You must be very smart to find my phone number."

"I touched the picture Mommy took of you and Adam, and you said hello."

His smile grew. JenniLynn had done the same thing he had. She'd taken a photo from their day of fishing and then made it his contact image. The feeling that swirled through his stomach was a dangerous one, but it probably meant nothing on her end.

"What can I help you with this evening?" he asked, amused by this little girl's gusto.

"I left my unicorn stuffie at your house. Can you—"

"Sasha Marie Garrett, who are you talking to now?" JenniLynn's exasperated tone in the background told him this might not be the first time her middle child had snuck her phone and made a call.

"I called Mr. Grayson."

"Go get back in bed, and I'll be there in a minute."

"Okay," Sasha said with a resigned sigh. "Bye-bye, Mr. Grayson."

"Goodnight, Sasha."

There was a jostling sound. "Hi, Grayson. I'm so sorry about this."

He chuckled and propped his bare feet on the coffee table. "No apology necessary. You've got a precocious one there."

"You're not telling me anything new. My sweet Sasha keeps me on my toes. Lila is Mommy's little helper, and Hallie is my calm child. Well, except on the unexpected occasions when she has a meltdown."

"It sounds to me like you're a lucky woman," he said, and then instantly worried she would think he was scolding her for not appreciating her girls. Her pause made him nervous, and unable to sit still, he stood and started down the hallway.

"You're right. I really am a lucky mom. I might be tired and ready for a bit of quiet, but I'm blessed."

The fact that she appreciated her situation made him like her even more. He wished his house was filled with the sound of children all year round. He looked into his son's bedroom and smiled at the sight of him curled up under the rocket ship bedspread. Pulling the door almost closed, he couldn't help thinking of his son's questions about more children.

"I love being a dad. I wish Adam was with me all the time." The words left his mouth before he thought about them. Why had he admitted that to someone he barely knew?

"I can imagine it's hard to be away from him. Adam is a really great kid. Did you see how sweet he was with Hallie? And all my girls, really."

"That's my boy." He had tried to instill caring values in his son since the day he was born. It was nice to know others saw and appreciated that fact. "I understand Sasha was supposed to be in bed?"

"You guessed it. I had already tucked her in with a story

and a song, my phone was charging on the kitchen counter, and I was in the…"

He knew what she wasn't saying, and wished she would hurry and say it, because while he waited, he was picturing her in a bubble bath.

JenniLynn couldn't tell him she'd been in the bathtub, again. He was going to think she was doing it on purpose as some lame way of tempting him. She searched her mind for something else to say but was coming up blank.

"JenniLynn? Did I lose you?"

"No. I'm still here."

"I think we lost connection for a minute. You were saying something about where you were, but I didn't hear the rest."

She sensed a bit of amusement in his voice and got the feeling he already knew the answer. "Did my child tell you where I was while she was making phone calls?"

He chuckled. "She might have mentioned something about singing and a bubble bath."

She groaned but then laughed. "Of course she did."

He made a throat-clearing noise, and she suspected he was trying not to laugh. "Your daughter seems to know the best times to find her opportunity for a late-night phone call."

"What am I in for when she's a teenager?"

"She'll probably be your most well-behaved child in her teenage years."

"Oh, so you're one of those wishful thinkers."

"I try to be."

JenniLynn had the urge to crawl into bed and keep talking to him, but she had things to tend to before she could rest. "I better go see if Sasha is still awake."

"I can bring her toy over to your place tomorrow."

"You don't have to go out of your way or rush to get it back to us. She has plenty more toys."

"It's no problem. Adam and I will be out and about and going right by your place. If you'll be home tomorrow afternoon?"

"We will be. I'm looking forward to a Sunday at home, even though I'll have to do a little bookkeeping and a few things outside."

"In that case, we'll see you midafternoon."

"The girls will be excited to see Adam. And you," she added, and heard his soft chuckle.

"I'm glad to hear it."

Why had she said that? She really needed to just stop talking. "Goodnight, Grayson."

"Goodnight, Mayor Jenni."

She smiled to herself. The way he'd said her name in his deep, smooth voice, it might as well have been a lover's caress. It felt like he was calling her sweetheart rather than a professional title.

When she went into the girls' room, Sasha's twin bed was empty. "Where is that child?" she whispered.

Lila was alone in her twin bed beneath her pink quilt, so she kissed the top of her head and went next door to see if her middle child had crawled in with Hallie. Her baby girl was alone in her crib. She looked so small with her knees tucked up under her tummy and her bottom up in the air. JenniLynn leaned down to kiss her forehead.

There was really only one place left that Sasha might be. Sure enough, she was stretched out like a starfish in the center of JenniLynn's king-size bed. She eased onto the bed beside her little girl. She looked so angelic in sleep, and all the frustration she'd felt after catching her on the phone vanished.

Her unexpected phone conversation with Grayson had turned out to be a pleasant surprise. Maybe she wasn't so upset with her mischievous child after all.

Something he'd said on the phone repeated in her mind. *I love being a dad. I wish Adam was with me all the time.*

As if she didn't already like Grayson more than she should, now he had to go and prove he was the kind of man who was unafraid to talk about feelings and wishes. A man who liked being a father. Unlike her ex-husband, Rob, who wasn't even capable of babysitting his own children without his parents' help.

She covered Sasha and kissed her rosy cheek. "I love you."

With her mind too wound up to fall asleep now, she grabbed a romance novel from her bedside table and opened it. It was safest to live vicariously through a fictional character and save a real-life romance for when her heart was healed and her mind was ready.

The sun was bright, and Grayson was ready for a fantastic day.

"Where are we going, Dad?" Adam asked for about the tenth time since they'd left Ambling Hills Ranch.

"I told you, it's a surprise."

"But I just can't wait. Tell me, please, please, please." He performed his best sad puppy-dog expression, making his big eyes appear even larger and his lower lip curled down, so much like one of his mother's looks.

Grayson's grin widened. His son's expression was very fitting because they were on their way to pick out a puppy. He had been waiting for Adam to be here for this day, and the age of the animals made it perfect timing. "We're almost there. You can wait two more minutes."

"Am I really gonna like the surprise?"

"I'm pretty sure I'll be dad of the year after this."

His truck tires rumbled over a cattleguard that led onto a new acquaintance's farm. Jay had a small animal rescue in a nearby town and a mama dog who'd given birth to five puppies. It was time for them to be adopted, and Adam was getting the first pick. There was a fenced area where dogs of all shapes, sizes and ages romped around in the sunshine.

"Wow! Look, Dad. They have lots of dogs." His eagerness dimmed as he sighed. "I wish Mom wasn't allergic to them."

"Me, too, kiddo. But thankfully, you and I are not allergic. That would make my surprise very difficult."

"Are we getting a dog?"

"We sure are."

"Woohoo," his son cheered, and tried to jump for joy but his seatbelt held him down. "Which one?"

"You get to pick," he said as he parked his truck beside a green tractor. "There are five puppies looking for a home."

Adam was out of the truck before Grayson could even get his seatbelt unbuckled. When he caught up to him, he was standing at the fence talking to several dogs who'd run over to check out the new person. He joined his son and waved to Jay, who motioned for them to come around to the gate.

The two men chatted while Adam played with all the puppies to see which one would be coming home with them.

"Dad, I think they will be sad to be separated. Maybe we should take all of them."

"Good try, kiddo, but that is a hard no to five dogs."

"Well, okay," he said skeptically. "It's going to be a really hard choice."

In the end, they drove away with two female pups. One

looked a lot like the golden retriever mom, and the other one looked as if she had a chocolate lab for a dad.

A short while later, Grayson and Adam arrived at Jenni-Lynn's place with their new canine family members. They each held one of the wiggly dogs as they went up onto the wide front porch of her white ranch house. He rang the bell, and her seven-year-old, Lila, opened the door. She saw the puppies and squealed.

He winced at the high-pitched sound.

"You have puppies!" she said.

"Want to come outside and play with them?" Adam asked.

Lila looked back over her shoulder and yelled, "Mommy, I'm going outside to play with Adam's puppies."

"Puppies?" said another familiar little voice right before Sasha popped her head around the corner with a beaming smile that made her look like a cherub. "I wanna play, too."

Lila and Adam were already headed into the yard, so he kneeled on the threshold to be at the little girl's level. "Hello, Sasha."

"Hi, Mr. Grayson." She held out her arms to take the small animal and gently cuddled him against her chest. "What's your puppy's name?"

"They don't have names yet. Maybe you can help Adam pick them."

Sasha tried to look under the pup she was holding. "Is it a boy or a girl?"

"They're both girls."

"Okay. I'll help him." Sasha nodded as if she was taking on an important job and talked to the pup on her way toward the other kids.

Still on one knee, he watched her go. The sound of footsteps caught his attention, and he turned his head back to the open doorway. The first thing he saw was a pair of blue jeans rolled up at the cuff and a pretty pair of feet with ruby-red toenails and red, white and blue flipflops. Very patriotic.

His smile grew as his gaze swept—not too slowly—up to JenniLynn's slightly bemused expression.

"Hello, Mayor Jenni."

Chapter Six

Grayson Abernathy's smile was so big that his eyes narrowed with amusement. The way he said her name—in a voice that was deep and penetrating—made JenniLynn shiver. This cowboy was a fine example of masculinity with plenty of playfulness, and an unexpected sweetness. Not to mention, handsome and a great dad.

Some might even say he was swoon-worthy.

Logically, she knew that he wasn't down on one knee to propose, but the visual made tingly sensations spiral through her body. Before any wild ideas took shape, it was best to play it off as the joking around that it was—rather than the unintended seduction it felt like.

"Mr. Abernathy." She dramatically clasped a hand to her heart and fluttered her lashes. "Down on one knee already? I hardly know you."

"Fair enough, ma'am." He chuckled and stood to his full height. "Hope you don't mind that we brought over our new pets? I should have called to check and see if it was okay."

"I don't mind at all. We lost our old dog last year, and I've been thinking of getting another." She motioned for him to take a seat on the front porch swing.

It rocked as they each sat on opposite ends. "If you're

serious, I know where you can get a puppy. There are two males and one female left from the same litter as ours."

"I might take you up on that." She sighed and stretched out her legs. "But the thought of house training a puppy is very daunting."

"They also have older dogs for adoption, and I bet some of them are house trained."

"That might be an idea." She glanced at the giggling kids then at him and pointed a finger. "But I have a suspicion that my girls are *now* going to want a puppy."

He grimaced. "Sorry about that. Where's Hallie?"

"She's napping, but I expect her to wake up any minute."

Children's laughter and excited barking and yipping filled the air as the three kids played with the puppies in the front yard. Grayson was clearly enjoying the relaxing moment as he sat on the swing beside her. Something her ex had never made time to do.

It should have been a wonderful moment to see her girls so happy, but there was a sudden pit in her stomach. A longing. Something that felt out of reach. Her heart felt heavy and achy. What was it that she was longing for? Maybe the feeling pressing in on her was the humiliation of being played for a fool by her own spouse.

She still had more healing to do.

"I'm pretty good at training dogs," Grayson said, and pushed his black cowboy boots against the porch, making the swing sway slowly back and forth. "If you end up with a puppy, I'll help you with the process. Since I'm to blame."

She eyed him, trying to judge if he was being serious. What exactly would that team project entail? What was he hoping to get out of this? It sounded like a lot of time spent together, and it made her nervous. She wasn't up for anything serious with a man. "I couldn't expect you to do that."

The screen door squeaked as it opened partway. Hallie peeked out, but she stopped when she saw Grayson. She rubbed her eye with a little fist like she always did when she was trying to wake up.

JenniLynn stood and held out a hand. "Come here, sweetie. Say hi to Mr. Grayson, and then we can go play with the puppies."

"Puppies?" the toddler whispered.

"Yes. Two little puppies that would love to meet you." She pointed to the other kids who were sitting under their big pine tree.

Hallie lifted her arms to be picked up, and JenniLynn scooped her onto her hip and then reached right inside the door to grab her daughter's pink boots. Once she had her shoes on, they joined the others.

Grayson followed them out into the front yard. "Any luck with names yet?" he asked his son.

"No names that sound right."

"I have good ideas," Sasha said. "The brown one can be Bling, and the gold one is Sparkle."

Adam shook his head and held the golden retriever close to his chest. "I am not naming a ranch dog Sparkle. You can save that name for your puppy."

She gasped and spun to face JenniLynn. "Are we getting a puppy?"

"I want a puppy," Lila said.

"Puppy?" Hallie chimed in.

She sighed as she smiled at her sweet girls, unable to resist them. "Yes. We're getting a puppy."

"Yay!"

"Thank you, Mommy."

Grayson looked at her with an I'm sorry expression. "I really will help with house training."

"I'll probably take you up on that if it comes to it." She lifted one of the puppies to brush her cheek against the soft fur.

A little later, they all walked closer to the barn so the girls could show Adam their chickens. Grayson and Jenni-Lynn each held a tired puppy while the kids had a contest to see who could catch the most chickens and get them put back into their coop the fastest. It was a hysterical competition with plenty of excitement and lots of noise. Because it was something Lila did all the time, she won. Adam was a very gracious loser and asked for tips on how to catch them.

At the corral that was connected to her barn, Grayson propped an arm across the top of the fence railing. "Wow. Nice bull."

"You really know how to compliment a girl."

He winced. "That sounded weird."

"If I wasn't raised on a ranch, I might think so." She grinned. "But I'll take it as the jealousy that it is."

He laughed, a deep resonant sound. "I can't deny I'm a bit jealous. I need to buy a new bull soon."

She rested one foot on the bottom railing of the corral. "He is a fine boy. I have him penned up because the vet is coming tomorrow for a routine check."

They spent a few minutes discussing veterinarians and the price of cattle, and he was able to make the boring topics entertaining. She might not be up for anything serious with a man, but keeping casual company with a nice guy didn't seem like too much to handle. They had a lot in common. They'd both grown up on ranches and shared a similar since of humor.

Adam came running up to them with a couple of chicken feathers sticking out of his hair and shirt pocket. "Dad, I'm hungry."

"Me, too." He plucked the feathers from his little chick's hair. "I guess we better get home and make dinner."

"Stay," JenniLynn said before even giving the offer a second thought. "I made a huge pot of chili, and I'm going to put cornbread and a batch of cookies into the oven."

Adam's face lit up. "The same kind of cookies you brought over yesterday?"

"The same ones."

"Yes! I love those cookies. Can we stay, Dad? Please."

"Sure. We can stay."

"Yippie." He turned and ran back toward her three girls, who were now on the front porch with the puppies.

"He's not a big fan of my cooking," Grayson admitted with a grin and shrug.

"I could trade you some easy recipes for puppy training."

"That is an interesting proposal." They walked back toward the house. "I can get on board with that."

"If you trained our puppy at your house with the other two, I might even consider cooking and freezing meals for you."

He shifted his hat. "Are you just trying to save your floors from puppy puddles?"

"Good thought," she said. "Thank you for pointing that out."

While she got cornbread into the oven, Grayson sat on a stool at the kitchen island and kept her company. The puppies napped in a box lined with a towel. Grayson noted Hallie sitting on the floor, rocking back and forth as she colored a picture of a flower.

"Kids, time to eat," she called to them in the family room.

The six of them sat around her dining table and filled their bowls and plates.

"That used to be my daddy's chair," Sasha said to Grayson.

JenniLynn sucked in a sharp breath. "Sasha."

"Would you like for me to move?" he asked the four-year-old. "I can switch with you or Adam."

"No. I think it's okay." Sasha sighed and shook her head. "He was a bad boy and made bad choices."

Adam looked at his dad with wide eyes, and he patted his son's arm and whispered that he would tell him later.

JenniLynn changed the subject by asking the kids what they wanted to do next weekend. Grayson gave her a knowing smile, and she appreciated his support.

Over the next few days, JenniLynn was super busy at work. A temp agency had sent her an assistant for the week, but unfortunately, the woman lived too far away for her to be a good long-term hire. She was counting on Grayson to find someone who would be a good fit.

She'd had several recent meetings about the Dinosaur Center and the dig. Things were moving along, but not as rapidly as she would have liked.

After a stressful meeting with the city council, JenniLynn sat in her desk chair, kicked off her heels and wiggled her toes. She'd had to deal with a few members of the council, like Billy Riley, who she always butted heads with. Unlike her, some of them came from long political backgrounds, and their ideas about how to serve the people, and not their own agendas, sometimes got in the way.

It had been a long day, and she was looking forward to heading home in another hour. Her phone rang, and she smiled when she saw the image of Grayson and Adam's smiling faces on the phone screen.

"Good afternoon, Mr. Abernathy. What can the mayor's office do for you today?"

He chuckled. "It's what I can do for you."

"Oh, good. Do tell." She scolded herself when her mind

drifted to things that weren't work related, such as fishing with the kids or dinner together.

"The consensus for Jobs Corps is to have training over several evening sessions," he said.

"That's perfect. I was hoping that would be the popular choice."

"Me, too. Did you see the dog training video I sent you?" Grayson asked.

He'd changed the topic as quickly as one of her kids, and she smiled to herself. It had become common for their professional conversations to become personal. "I did. It was very helpful."

If her instincts were correct, he was looking for excuses to call her. Just like she was doing.

The next afternoon, Grayson patted the small red and white calf, and it kicked up its back hooves as it ran off to join its mother. After almost six months, his animals had settled in well on the new spread. Inhaling a deep breath of fresh air, he studied the thick grass beneath his boots. The recent rains had really helped it sprout.

His phone rang, and he smiled when he saw that it was JenniLynn calling.

"Hello, Mayor. It is you, right?"

Her pretty laughter came over the line. "Yes, it's me this time."

"What can I do for you today?"

"We've decided that it's time for the Garrett girls to get our puppy."

"That's great. I know the girls are thrilled."

"They are. I was thinking, since you know the guy and where he lives and everything, maybe you want to go along. Or you can just give me directions if you're too busy."

"I'd love to go." He'd said it so quickly that he sounded like a desperate teenager. "Adam will be excited to go."

Way to blame it on your kid.

He rolled his eyes at himself. Why did this woman and the thought of seeing her again make him so excited and nervous?

"Good. I'm glad you two can join us."

"I would drive, but I can't fit all six of us in my truck. We'll have to take your SUV."

"That's okay. We'll pick you up. Can you go tomorrow?"

"Yes, we can. I'll give Jay a call and tell him we're coming. And I'll let you know what time after I talk to him." He started walking back to the house where Adam was feeding the puppies in the backyard. "I forgot to ask, how was yesterday's meeting with the city council guy who always disagrees with you?"

"Basically, a waste of my time. I think he just likes to be ornery so we have to schedule another meeting. I guess it makes him feel important."

"Maybe he just likes spending time with you." *Like I do*, he added silently.

She made a dismissive sound. "I don't think so. I'm always cordial to him, but I never encourage him in any way, shape or form."

"Some people are hardheaded."

"Then I'll just keep hammering the message until he gets it," she said.

He laughed and pictured her in one of her power suits with her hands on her hips. He loved a fierce woman. "Good for you."

"You don't seem very hardheaded."

"Only when I have to be."

He wondered if she had any idea how attractive men

found her. From the little bit he'd gathered about her ex-husband, she probably had no idea what a desirable woman she was. And it wasn't all about her pretty face or nice body. JenniLynn radiated something special that he'd been immediately drawn to. It made him want to be around her.

He heard crying in the background. "Is someone hurt?"

"No. That Sasha's mad cry, not the I'm-hurt cry. But… I still need to go deal with it."

"I'll call you later about a time for tomorrow."

"I'm looking forward to it."

"Good. I'll call around bathtime."

Her pretty laughter drifted over the phone line. "Bye, Grayson."

He grinned as he hung up and then walked over to Adam. "Hey, buddy. Good job with all of your chores this afternoon."

"I'm getting faster and stronger every day."

"You sure are getting stronger. Just remember not to rush, because that's how you get hurt. You can take your time and do it right. That's more important."

"Okay, Dad."

"Want to go back to Jay's farm tomorrow and help the Garrett girls pick out a puppy of their own?"

"Sure. I like seeing all the different dogs. Is Ms. Jenni-Lynn going to cook for us again?"

He chuckled, because he'd had the same thought. "I don't know about that, but she did promise to give me some recipes."

"She better give you some cooking classes, too." Adam picked up one of the dog toys and tossed it into the air before catching it.

His son was thinking along the same lines as he was, but Grayson's motivation was to spend time with JenniLynn, while his son's enthusiasm was inspired by his stomach. "That means we will have to hang out with the girls more."

"That's okay. They're pretty fun to hang out with."

His thoughts exactly.

Chapter Seven

Even with all the excited anticipation of getting a new pet, Hallie fell asleep in the car on the way to the farm. "Wake up, sweet girl," JenniLynn crooned. "We're here."

"No," Hallie whimpered. She arched her back before hiding her face.

"Don't cry." Lila kissed her baby sister's cheek. "We're getting a puppy!"

"Lila and Sasha, why don't you girls come with me and Adam," Grayson said. "We can meet some of the dogs and give your little sister a few minutes to wake up."

JenniLynn mouthed a thank-you to Grayson. His sexy wink-and-grin combo made warmth bloom in her cheeks. He gathered the kids and gave her a bit of quiet to tend to her grumpy toddler.

She stroked her daughter's soft curls and watched the four of them walking toward a big red barn with a connected fenced area. Sasha reached for Grayson's hand as she skipped along beside him, and he gently held her tiny fingers as if it came completely naturally. Her heart melted a little bit. He did come from a big family and probably had lots of experience with kids of all ages.

Grayson had known she needed a quiet minute with her cranky toddler, almost as if without saying a word, they were working as a team. She hadn't counted on parenting all alone, and it was nice to have backup. She'd had to tell Rob *specifically* what she needed help with—even when it was something as routine as bedtime.

But Grayson just seemed to know. How nice it would be to have a partner who knew how to work as a team. Someone who actually knew what the word *partner* meant. She and Grayson were both single adults and— She squeezed her eyes closed and cut off the thought.

What is wrong with me? I'm getting way out ahead of my skis.

She shouldn't be having these thoughts about a man she barely knew. A man she liked and respected. And was very attracted to. She rested her cheek on her daughter's head.

There were perfectly understandable reasons why she was having these thoughts. She was parenting alone, and it was scary to be the only one in charge. And yes, she was lonely. It had been a long time since she had been held by a man. Long before her divorce. She wanted it all. A partner to parent with, an attentive husband who was also a friend. And a lover.

She couldn't risk Grayson becoming a rebound relationship. She liked him too much to risk wrecking the friendship growing between them by jumping into something she wasn't ready for. And she didn't want her children to get caught up in her mistake.

"I'm just looking for an ideal dream, but I need to be realistic," she said on a long sigh.

Hallie looked up at her and cocked her head as if trying to figure out what her mommy was talking about.

"Hey, sweetie. I'm going to get you out of your seat, but I'll carry you until you can wake up." She unbuckled the car seat and lifted her into her arms. Hallie rested her head on her shoulder with a sigh, and she patted her tiny back then hurried to catch up with the others. "I think I know something that will improve your mood."

Grayson and the kids were talking to a man who must be Jay. The man's thick, gray hair stood straight up on top and the creases in his face indicated he smiled often. He waved to her, and they were introduced, while Hallie hid her face against JenniLynn's neck.

"Can I take them to see the puppies?" Adam asked Jay.

"Sure. They're right through that white door. They are napping in a kennel, but you can go get them out to play and see which one strikes your fancy."

Hallie wanted to get down, so JenniLynn put her toddler on her feet. Rather than following the excited older kids, Hallie plopped down onto her bottom in the soft grass. Adam, Lila and Sasha went through a doorway, and a golden retriever came out before the door closed.

JenniLynn bent to pick up Hallie, but she fussed and refused, crossing her little arms over her chest. "I think she still needs a minute to wake up," she told Grayson.

"No problem. I'll go with the other kids."

"That would be great. Otherwise, they might come out thinking they can have all the puppies." She sat on the grass beside Hallie and brushed back a curl that was stuck to her daughter's damp cheek.

"Hello, beautiful," Grayson said.

Feeling a touch of jealousy, she looked up to see who it was that he found beautiful, and she smiled when she saw him petting the golden retriever that had come out of the barn where the kids were. As he moved on toward the doorway, she let herself enjoy watching him walk away. His jeans fit perfectly. So well, in fact, he could be in an ad campaign, becoming the world's next famous denim-covered backside.

She smiled to herself and rubbed gentle circles on Hallie's back to soothe her. The golden retriever started toward them.

"She's very friendly," the farmer called out to her. "She's the mama."

The mother dog slowly and carefully approached them and sniffed her toddler's foot.

Hallie looked up, and her toothy smile bloomed. "Doggie."

Moving in with caution, the sweet animal gently placed her chin on Hallie's little lap. Her sweet girl smiled and buried her fingers in the golden fur, and in response, the dog sighed with contentment. Footsteps caught JenniLynn's attention, and she looked up as someone approached.

"That's Sandy," Jay said. "She's a sensitive dog and seems to know when someone is upset."

"She certainly turned my daughter's mood around in a hurry."

"Sandy was in training to be a Seeing Eye dog, but she didn't make the cut because it turns out she has poor vision in one eye. But she has a lot of good therapy dog skills, and she's also available for adoption."

"That's good to know. She seems like a sweetheart."

"She is."

JenniLynn watched her toddler kiss the top of the dog's head. "Is she house trained?"

"Yes, she's very well trained and fantastic with kids."

Her quiet child was babbling to the dog, and JenniLynn made a spur of the moment decision. "Hallie, would you like this pretty dog to come home with us? To live at our house?"

"My doggie." She leaned forward and hugged the animal's neck.

JenniLynn smiled at Jay. "I think that's a yes."

"Great. Are you still taking a puppy, too?"

"Yes, I'm pretty sure we will be leaving with a puppy as well. If we take Sandy, will her puppies be okay without her?"

"They sure will. I have some friends who are taking whichever two puppies you don't take. They'll have a good home."

"Oh, that's great. It's kind of nice that the whole litter is going to a home with a sibling or their mom."

He smiled at her and nodded. "That's a nice way to look at it. I'll go get a few things together and be back in a couple of minutes with the paperwork."

Grayson strode toward them. "What did I miss?"

Hallie clapped her hands. "Doggie."

"I see that doggie has made you a happy girl." He squatted beside them, and Hallie grabbed his thumb and pulled his hand over to pet the mama dog, though she didn't make eye contact with him.

"Sandy and Hallie have bonded, and she is coming home with us. She has therapy dog training, and she seemed to know Hallie was upset and needed comfort."

"That's wonderful." He smiled, but there was a curious expression she couldn't place on his handsome face as he looked at Hallie and the dog.

"Did the girls pick a puppy?"

"They sure did. He's a cutie and looks like a mix between a golden retriever and a lab. They're letting it say goodbye to the last two puppies. Did Jay tell you the good news about house training?"

"No. Tell me."

"He's been working with all of the puppies, and although they aren't fully house broken yet, they're making good progress."

"Excellent news." She leaned closer to Grayson. "You'll still give me some guidance, right?"

He reached out like he might touch her, but his hand changed direction midair, and he shifted his Stetson. "Yes, of course."

Her relief was mixed with an uncomfortable sensation she couldn't name at first, but then it came to her. She needed to be careful about how much trust and dependance she put in Grayson. She had to count on herself first and foremost.

Adam and the girls came outside, and Lila had a fluffy tan puppy in her arms. Sasha, not to be left out, had a protective hand on the animal's back.

"What about the other two puppies?" Lila asked as she looked wistfully back over her shoulder at the barn. "They'll be lonely."

"Don't you worry about them," Jay said. "My friends are adopting both of them. I'll be taking them over to their house right after you leave. They will get to stay together and won't be lonely."

Lila hugged her puppy closer. "We'll make sure you're not lonely, either."

Jay grinned, making his wrinkles deepen. "You are just like your mom. She was worried about them, too."

"That doesn't surprise me," Grayson said. "The Garrett girls are a sweet bunch."

"I'm sweet," Sasha proclaimed with her best smile.

"You sure are." Grayson tugged gently on one of her braids. "Your mama is a great role model."

JenniLynn blushed under his praise. "Lila, Sasha, come meet Sandy. She will also be coming home with us."

"For real, Mommy?"

"Yes, sweetie." She returned Lila's hug.

Her two oldest dropped down onto the grass beside their

sister and showered their new dog with attention. The puppy crawled out of Lila's arms and rooted around on his mama's tummy. Adam joined in on the canine and kid pile-up.

"Oh, my." JenniLynn smiled at Grayson. "That is a lot of energy. What have I done?"

"It looks to me like you've made your children very happy." He wrapped an arm around her shoulders and squeezed.

It felt so good to be held against his side, but too soon, he dropped his arm as if he shouldn't be touching her.

With two new family members, they loaded back into her SUV. Her two youngest were in the middle row with Sandy at their feet. Adam and Lila were in the third row with the puppy. On the drive home, there was a rowdy discussion about the new puppy's name.

"I want to name him Sparkle," Sasha said from her booster seat.

"But he's a boy dog," Adam said.

"You can call the mama dog Sparkle," Lila suggested to her sister.

"No, no, no," Sasha said. "Her name is Sandy."

In the front passenger seat, Grayson chuckled at the interaction.

JenniLynn stopped at a red light. "I have an idea. If the mama dog's name is Sandy Sparkle, then the boy puppy's last name can also be Sparkle."

Grayson shifted in the seat to look over his shoulder at the kids. "You just need a good first name that goes well with the last name Sparkle."

"Sparky Sparkle," her middle child said with a delighted giggle.

"I like that name," Lila agreed.

Grayson chuckled and turned back to the front windshield with a satisfied smile. "Looks like that's settled."

"Good teamwork," she said, and then instantly held her breath, worried it had sounded like she was calling them a couple. Grayson didn't seem to notice, so she relaxed. It was nice to have another adult around at times like this, but she would have to be very careful and not allow herself to take advantage of him just because he made her life easier. "What did you end up naming your puppies?"

"You know how Adam has a love for space? I'm the proud owner of Moon and Star."

"I like it. Easy, one-syllable and they sound good together."

"It sounds like my ranch dogs were named by someone who attended Woodstock."

"At least one of them isn't named Rainbow River Rock."

That made him laugh. "True."

"Just wait until Sasha finds out and tags on a last name for your dogs, too. Moon Sparkle and Star Sparkle," she said quietly enough for only him to hear.

His mouth turned up into a big grin. "Since our ranches almost touch, when the puppies are all grown, all the dogs will probably meet up in the middle. We'll have the only two ranches patrolled by a family of dogs known as the Sparkle Bunch."

They shared a smile that made butterflies dance in her belly. JenniLynn glanced in the rearview mirror, and she couldn't help but wistfully wonder what it might be like to become the Garrett and Abernathy bunch.

Chapter Eight

When they got back to Grayson's house, the kids insisted that Sandy and Sparky Sparkle had to say hello to Moon and Star.

They went around to his backyard where he'd built a dog run, complete with a cozy little house, sunny areas and plenty of shady ones. They were safe from predators and had indoor and outdoor spaces to run, play and sleep when they weren't in the house.

He hooked his thumbs in the front pockets of his blue jeans. "Want me to throw some hamburgers on the grill while the kids and dogs play?"

JenniLynn bit her lip as if it was a tough decision, but then she nodded as she seemed to make up her mind and smiled at him. "I guess we could do that."

He reminded himself that she was not ready for a romantic relationship, and neither was he. He just needed to be her friend and put aside his attraction to her. "The kids can play while I give you some puppy training tips."

"That's a good idea."

"Adam," he called out to his son. "I'm going to go inside to prep some food."

His son stopped, tilted his head and gave him a suspicious look. "You're cooking?"

He heard JenniLynn chuckle behind him. "I'm grilling burgers and hot dogs."

"Oh, that's good. We're safe if you're cooking meat outside." He spun around and then went back to playing.

"Stay inside the fenced area, please," he told the children.

"Okay, Dad."

"Okay, Mr. Grayson."

JenniLynn was grinning at him when he turned around. "You *really* can't cook?"

He shrugged and returned her good humor. "Most people seem to think so. I do tend to cook on the grill a lot."

"Well, your son seems to think we're safe, so I'm happy. I'm pretty good in the kitchen, but I never cook on the grill. I find it intimidating."

"Looks like we have opposite skills sets. I can teach you how to use the barbeque grill."

"Thanks," she said. "I've been putting together some simple-to-make recipes for you."

"Are you going to teach me how to make them?" he asked, really hoping she'd say yes.

"I think we can work that into the agreement. I can give you some pointers in the kitchen along with the recipes."

"Sounds like a good deal to me." It would be a test of his willpower to spend this much time with her, but he couldn't resist the opportunity.

"Let me check on the girls, and then I'll come inside and help you."

"Take your time."

In his kitchen, he pulled out all the ingredients from the refrigerator and pantry and piled them all on the granite countertop. Hot dog and hamburger buns, meat, veggies, condiments, chips and his special seasoning blend.

He turned on the water to wash his hands before seasoning and making hamburger patties. Through the kitchen window, he watched JenniLynn interacting with the children. Four kids and four dogs were creating a happy noise, and she was laughing. It was clear she loved being a mom.

He sighed. "Why am I torturing myself by spending so much time with her?"

The answer came to him instantly. Because they had a lot in common and shared values that made her fun to be around. She was entertaining to talk to, and he couldn't deny the fact that JenniLynn Garrett was a pleasure to look at. But mostly, it was the way she calmed some of the chaos in his mind.

Her shoulder-length blond hair was loose and dancing around her face as she moved. Her pink sundress and white sneakers that were studded with rhinestones were a cute combination. She was feminine in her frilly dress but also ready to break into a run to protect her girls if needed. He chuckled and dried his hands. With the amount of bling on JenniLynn's shoes, it was no wonder Sasha talked about sparkles.

Instead of getting to work, he continued to watch all of them run around his new backyard. Hearing Adam's laughter lightened his worries. JenniLynn's joy showed in the way she moved, and he suspected the sadness only made an appearance when she was alone. He'd seen the way a mention of her ex or their divorce made a flicker of something painful flash in her expression before she could mask it. If his intuition was right, she was hiding much of her pain and sadness deep down on the inside.

She turned and caught him watching, so rather than try to duck or pretend he hadn't been gawking, he waved but then turned away. "I'm such a dork. I need a beer."

He chose a beer from a local brewery. The bottle cap

came off with a satisfying pop and fizz, and he was taking his first sip as she came through the doorway.

"Everyone is hungry," she said as she closed the kitchen door.

"It won't take long to cook. Would you like something to drink?"

"I'll have what you're having." She propped a hand on the counter and looked at the pile of food. "What can I do to help you?"

"Can you wash and prep the veggies while I season the meat?" He handed her a cold drink.

"I sure can. Cheers." She clinked her bottle against his and took a sip. "First, I hope you don't mind if I organize everything we'll be working with. It helps me work better."

"Be my guest." He stepped out of her way and drank his beer with a grin.

"It's your first cooking lesson. When things are orderly, it helps you work better."

It was something he taught his neurodivergent clients, and he really should take his own advice. "Noted."

She grabbed the chips and buns and laid them out in a neat line on another section of the counter, lined up the condiments, and put the meat on one side of the sink and the veggies on the other. "There. Isn't that better?"

"Much," he said and tried not to laugh. He had enjoyed every minute of her preparation.

"Now I just need a cutting board and a knife."

"In that drawer." They started working together on each side of the apron-front kitchen sink, and he liked the company.

She cut a couple slices of the onion, and only a few seconds later, her eyes started to water. "Oh, my gosh, I can't see at all." Tears dripped down both cheeks. "I need to wash my hands so I can wipe my eyes."

"Hold still and I'll help. I already have clean hands." He grabbed a fresh hand towel and cupped one side of her face as he gently dabbed at her eyes. He couldn't resist stroking her cheek with his thumb. Her skin was so soft, and he wanted to linger and explore. He wanted so badly to kiss her lips.

"Thank you," she said in a soft voice.

He forced himself to let go and quickly turned on the water.

JenniLynn misjudged where it was and knocked over the bottle of hand soap. "Oh, fiddlesticks. Did I break anything?"

"Nope. All good. Let me help you." He took her hands in his and drew them into the stream of water, and without thinking about what he was doing, he added a squirt of soap and started washing her hands.

She caught her breath and then sighed and swayed in his direction. Their fingers were slipping and sliding. Tangling as they explored the shape of one another's hands. Heat pulsed up his arms and into his body.

He jolted, suddenly realizing what he was doing. He turned off the water, grabbed the towel and handed it to her without a word.

His impulsive handwashing had been inappropriate. He hadn't meant for it to turn into a seduction, but controlling himself in her company was proving to be a major challenge.

"You can massage my hands anytime you want," she said with a teasing grin and then rubbed her watery eyes. "You have strong fingers, and my hands always carry tension."

"Good to know." The fact that she seemed to be flirting rather than mad wasn't helping his self-control. Relief spread through him that she wasn't offended by his forwardness, but now he was thinking about doing it again.

"I can't remember the last time I had a full body massage, but I sure could use one." She kneaded the small of her back as if to demonstrate her need.

He internally groaned, but he saw the perfect excuse to touch her again. "You have makeup on your cheek." With his fingertips, he slowly wiped away the smudge of mascara. "You are so beautiful."

Her hands went to each side of his waist. They were close. So close. When she pressed her top teeth into her plump lower lip, his willpower withered, and he dipped his head until his mouth was a breath from hers, but he was still sensible enough to wait for her reaction before kissing her.

She slid her arms around his waist and pressed closer. "Grayson," she whispered.

The sound of his name ended with the warm, spicy sensation of her lips on his. Tender. Sensual. Electric.

But then suddenly, she pulled back with a soft gasp and pressed her fingertips to her lips.

Grayson's stomach dropped to his toes.

Chapter Nine

JenniLynn's heart was pounding, and her breath was coming too fast and not filling up her lungs. Even though she was officially single, in the middle of a beautiful kiss with Grayson, she'd been hit with an overwhelming sense that she was cheating.

"I'm sorry," Grayson said. The devastated expression on his face proved his statement. "I shouldn't have done that. I told myself I wouldn't."

"You didn't do anything wrong. I just got…" She took his hand in hers. "I had this freaky moment where it flashed through my mind that I was cheating. You're the first man since…" She let her words trail off again.

He squeezed her hand. "Hey, I understand. You don't have to say any more."

Looking into his blue eyes, she felt a sense of calm wash over her. "I appreciate that."

"You need a friend, and I can be that. I really can control myself."

"I have no doubt." When he opened his arms to offer a hug, she stepped into his friendly embrace. Resting her head on his chest felt nice. He was so much bigger than she was, with broad shoulders and height that allowed her to easily fit under his Stetson without bumping it with her head. She released a long, slow breath.

Grayson might be able to control himself, but with the tingles she was feeling, the real question was, could she?

She liked being around this man because he made her feel safe. Something she hadn't felt in quite some time.

"You take all the time you need," he said. "Don't rush yourself."

With her ear against his chest, his deep voice was a pleasant rumble that seemed to echo. She lifted her head and patted the spot right over his heart. "Thank you for being so understanding."

"You've got it."

They stepped apart at the same time, and she smoothed the front of her dress. "We better get this food cooked before we are mobbed by four hungry children. But I am not cutting anymore onion."

He grinned. "Noted. That can be my job from now on."

"Deal." This agreement made it sound like there would be more meals cooked together. But wasn't that what friends did? And she had promised to teach him. She switched to slicing tomatoes and glanced out the window to check on the kids. They were all still happily playing in the fenced yard.

Grayson covered the tray of prepared meat with a sheet of foil. "You do know that you didn't do anything wrong. Don't you?"

"I know. I guess our…kiss was just a shock to my system. A good one," she added quickly with a shy smile.

"I'm glad to hear it, and I couldn't agree more, but the speed and depth of our friendship is in your hands."

"My reaction is likely because earlier today I found out the date of Rob's trial for ballot tampering, and ever since, he's been on my mind."

"Will you have to testify?"

"I don't know for sure. I definitely won't be there in a supportive role, and I am not looking forward to the trial, but I do want it done so I can put it behind me. I want to feel like I'm completely free to move forward with my life."

"That's understandable. I'm assuming your husband was not supportive of you running for mayor?"

She shook her had as she arranged the lettuce leaves on a plate. "Rob was supportive, at first. Or so I thought. His enthusiasm quickly waned. Turns out, he never thought anyone would take my campaign seriously. He never expected I would be successful. I was just a stay-at-home mom who helped out on the ranch."

Grayson scowled. "At what point did his enthusiasm wane?"

She stared up at the ceiling as she thought about it. "It didn't take that long."

"Can I say what I'm thinking?" he asked.

"Absolutely." She put down the knife and faced him. "After the year I've had, honesty is refreshing."

"I'm going to guess it was about the time when you weren't home to…" Grayson scratched his head. "How do I put it?"

She suddenly knew what he was trying to say, and it made her stomach roll, and her jaw tighten. "When I wasn't home catering to his needs?"

"So, my feeling about him is right?"

"I guess it is. What business did I have trying to make my town better when I had a husband to please, a home to run and kids to take care of."

"I'm sorry, Jenni." He squeezed her shoulder. "You didn't deserve that."

Briefly, she tilted her head to rest her cheek on his hand.

The warmth and strength felt good, but the timing for a new relationship was all wrong. She needed to focus on her job and her kids. But Grayson's steadiness was so appealing.

"How did Rob get caught?"

"It was a series of events that led to the discovery of a text chain between the mayor-elect Marty Moore and Rob. Then a box of paper ballots was found hidden in a local warehouse. Marty was so scared in police custody that he spilled the beans on the whole scheme." She'd been so shocked and completely devastated, and the pain was still fresh enough to make her pulse rate skyrocket. "I filed for divorce as soon as I discovered what he'd done."

"Good for you. I'm glad you did."

"I hate that it has been so hard on my girls. Lila is quieter, Sasha is more needy and Hallie has slid backward in some of her milestones, like her speech. But… I know we'll be okay."

He sidestepped close enough to gently bump his shoulder against hers. "I sense a strength in your girls that matches yours. They are lucky to have you as their mother."

"I'm the one who got lucky. God sent me perfect, precious babies," she said.

"He sure did." Grayson picked up the metal tray. "Now let's take the burgers and hot dogs to the grill, and I'll show you how easy it is to cook outside."

Of course, JenniLynn had watched people cook on a grill or barbeque pit many times before, but she'd never done it herself. She didn't even have one at her house. He was right that it wasn't hard, and their meal was ready in no time.

"Do you want to eat outside?" he asked. "I just got this new picnic table, and it's big enough to fit all six of us."

"That's a great idea. The weather is too nice to eat indoors. I'll go gather everything up and bring it outside."

"There are paper plates in the pantry."

"I'll grab those, too." She went to the edge of the back patio. "Lila, will you help bring some things out to the picnic table, please?"

"Coming, Mommy." Her oldest ran over to her side, and Adam followed.

"I'll help, too, Ms. JenniLynn."

"Thank you, Adam."

They had everything outside in no time, and they all sat down to eat at the wooden table that was sheltered under the covered patio.

"Since the mama dog and her boy puppy will be at our house, and the two girl puppies will be here at your house, they should have playdates," Lila suggested as she swallowed a bite of her hot dog.

She and Grayson shared a smile, and she wondered if he was thinking what she was thinking. That she would like to have more playdates with him.

"How often should they get to play together?" Adam asked. "Every day?"

"Every day might be a little hard to pull off," Grayson said. "We live close, but it's not exactly next door."

JenniLynn wiped ketchup from Hallie's cheek. "If there was a gate between your ranch and Mr. Smith's ranch, like I have, you could drive to our house through the properties without even getting on the road."

Grayson looked thoughtfully in that direction as he chewed. "Or I could just buy his piece of property if he really does decide to sell."

"I'm pretty sure he will. You should talk to him about it and tell him you are interested. That might make the worry and hassle of putting it on the market not seem so daunting to him."

"I might do that." Grayson put down his cheeseburger. "When we're finished eating, how about we all get a lesson in house training puppies?"

"Are you a teacher?" Lila asked him.

"Not really. But I do volunteer as a job coach for teens and adults who need a little extra support."

"That's cool," her oldest daughter said, and then crunched into a potato chip.

"That reminds me," Grayson said to JenniLynn. "I have some more ideas for the Tenacity Job Corps to discuss with you."

"Oh, good. And I have some thoughts about how to make the bootcamp fun."

"Excellent," he said and looked around at the kids and dogs with a smile. "But it can wait until later so we can focus on this rowdy bunch."

JenniLynn laughed. "The Rowdy Bunch. I like that nickname."

"Mommy, do we have dog food?" Sasha asked.

"Yes. I bought some the last time I was at the store, along with all the puppy supplies."

"Can I be in charge of feeding them?" Lila asked.

"Absolutely. I expect lots of help at home from my big girls."

"I'm a big girl," Sasha said.

"You sure are, sweetie. Now sit down on your bottom."

Instead of listening, Sasha patted Grayson's shoulder with a sticky hand. "And you're a big boy."

JenniLynn almost spit out her sip of water but managed to swallow before laughing.

Grayson only shrugged and shot JenniLynn a sexy grin that made her cheeks warm.

* * *

After a very entertaining meal at his new picnic table and a puppy training lesson for everyone, JenniLynn insisted on helping him clean up before they left. He washed dishes while she put leftovers into plastic containers.

The back door opened, and Sasha came rushing into the kitchen. "Mommy, I've gotta go potty."

"Okay. Come this way." JenniLynn led her toward the half bathroom.

Grayson looked out the window to check on the rest of the kids. Lila was sitting with the mama dog, and Adam was holding Hallie's hand as they followed the puppies. His son was so good with the shy little girl, and Hallie was finally warming up to them.

But there was something bothering Grayson. Her limited speech concerned him, especially now that JenniLynn had mentioned a regression. There were a few other things he'd noticed, like the way she lined up toys without playing with them, rocked to self-soothe and consistently avoided eye contact, but perhaps he didn't know the toddler well enough to judge. Maybe he was just making too much out of a few behaviors. Hallie was only two, and he needed more time to observe. He'd wait for a sign that he should say something to JenniLynn about his concerns.

He continued to watch the kids, and the scene made him smile, reminding him of his own childhood with lots of siblings. But it also made the ache for more children grow stronger. He wanted a big, loud, two-parent family with a woman who loved him enough to share his life through all the ups and downs. Not just a good friend like Rebecca had been.

Familiar tension banded his chest. His fear of getting

it right the next time had kept him from fully opening his heart again.

His son deserved to have siblings, but these three little girls weren't his. He could not let himself start pretending they could be. JenniLynn was a woman who was in a rough place in her life, and she didn't need to deal with his baggage as well. Not to mention that her sweet little girls were also going through a rough time. He could only imagine how hard it was for them.

"All done," Sasha said as she ran by on her way to the door. "See you later, alligator."

He leaned a hip against the countertop and smiled at JenniLynn. "Has she been a fireball since birth?"

"Pretty much. Sasha hit most of her milestones early. Walking at ten months, and she has always been a chatterbox. It took a while before we could understand what she was saying, but that never stopped her."

This gave him the opening he needed to ask more about Hallie's speech. "Did Lila also talk early?"

JenniLynn paused with her hands on a plastic lid. "She was more average in her milestones. Why do you ask?"

"I just haven't heard Hallie say more than a couple of words, and you mentioned her regression."

Her brow furrowed, and she snapped the lid on the container. "She's just shy and has been through a lot of changes since…"

"You're right. What do I know?" he said. "If she's hitting all her milestones and her doctor is happy, just ignore me."

She chewed her thumbnail. "We didn't talk about her speech at her last visit. But it's been a rough year. My divorce has been really hard on the girls, and Hallie has two sisters who talk for her."

"You've all been through a lot lately." His goal was not

to upset her, so he decided to leave it at that. And change the subject. "Would you like help building a dog run like I have?"

"Really? Did you build it yourself?"

"I had some help, but mostly I did."

"That's impressive. My backyard is fenced, but I don't have a doghouse or anywhere to protect them from predators. After we lost our old dog, the house it slept in was so rundown that we threw it away."

"We can take a look at the areas of your yard that you're thinking might work. The next time our pets have a playdate," he said.

The corners of her mouth turned up into a big smile that mirrored his. "It's a plan. Next playdate at my house. I think we're starting to figure out how to be…friends."

"I believe you're right." It was true, but the word "friends" brought back a touch of tension.

"Do we need guidelines?" she asked. "Like not being alone in a room for too long?"

"Only if that's something you want." He sure wasn't looking forward to strict rules between them.

She shook her head. "No. That's completely silly. We're not teenagers."

"We definitely are not."

"Don't listen to me, Grayson. I haven't dated in a really long time." Her lips instantly formed an O, as if she'd said something wrong. "I didn't mean… Oh, smudge."

He hid his amusement of her word choice and took both of her hands in his. "JenniLynn, you don't have to watch what you say with me. I understand exactly what you're saying, and I want you to feel free to tell me what you are thinking any time you want to. I'm not going to judge you."

She brought their joined hands up to chest level as she stepped closer. "That is a really great offer. It means a lot."

With a gentle squeeze of his hands, she let go, and he instantly missed the contact. Resisting her charms was tough, but he would do whatever she needed. As he'd told her, he would let her steer the direction of their relationship.

"I need to get the girls home." She grabbed her big pink purse from the counter and put it over her shoulder. "Thank you for dinner. And for helping us get our two new family members."

"You're very welcome. It was a fun day." He opened the back door. "Let me help you get your half of the Rowdy Bunch into the car."

They rounded up the kids and dogs and after everyone said goodbye, they were ready to go.

"See you later, big boy," JenniLynn said quietly enough for only his ears, and then she got into her car.

This pretty woman was going to unintentionally kill him with her natural playfulness. It was the best kind of flirting. But he was up for resisting her...if it meant spending time together.

Chapter Ten

The workday was done, and JenniLynn was satisfied with all she had accomplished, but she'd been sitting all day long and felt stiff. She needed to stretch her legs, so rather than driving over to pick up the girls, she decided to walk. Since she was wearing slacks, she kicked off her high heels and put on the walking shoes she always carried in her car and took off toward the library to pick up the girls where their babysitter Courtney had taken them after picking them up from daycare. In an attempt to get in a bit of cardio, Jenni-Lynn kept a steady pace down Central Avenue.

"Mayor Garrett, can we talk to you?"

She stopped and turned to see two teenage girls in front of Tenacity Grocery. One was tall with dark curly hair and deep dimples. The other was petite and wearing a turquoise sundress that looked fabulous with her long red hair and matching freckles. "Hello, ladies. What can I do for you this evening?"

The tall one spoke up first. "We think you're so cool, and we want to get a photo with you for our social media."

"Would you be okay with that?" asked the other girl.

"Absolutely. I'm honored." This kind of thing happened more than she'd imagined it would. Not that she'd ever imagined having fans at all, but it surprised her how often women of all ages wanted to congratulate her on being the first female mayor of Tenacity.

With one of them on each side of her, they took a selfie beside the benches that lined the front of the century-old two-story brick building. The bottom floor housed the grocery store, and the top floor had rooms for rent. Locals loved to sit on the benches and chat as they watched the world go by. Rough wooden signs dangled from the second-floor balcony, announcing *Beer! Ice! Wine!* and giving the old place a back-in-time look and feel.

"Thank you so much, Mayor Garrett."

"You're welcome. Don't forget to tag me in your posts."

"We won't," they echoed in chorus.

Continuing her walk, she waved to several people and spoke to a few others. She should have known she couldn't get down the street without talking to people.

Now, she was running late to pick up the girls. Ella McIntyre, the town librarian, had offered to take care of them during story and art hour so Courtney could attend a family event. Ella's help had enabled her to have a meeting JenniLynn had been struggling to fit in because of schedule conflicts. But she didn't want to take advantage of the other woman's kindness.

A cool blast of air hit her as she pulled back the library door. Her girls were sitting together at a table covered with sheets of newspaper and painting wooden stars.

She waved to Ella, who was putting bottles of paint into a tub of art supplies. "Thank you so much for offering to stay late with my girls."

"I'm glad to help out. I enjoy spending time with the three of them."

"Hi, girls. Can you start cleaning up so Ms. Ella can get out of here?"

"Hi, Mommy," Lila said.

"Mommy, look what I made." Sasha held up her star, right on brand with lots of sparkly red glitter.

"Beautiful. You all did a wonderful job."

"You can leave your stars here to dry and pick them up next week," Ella said.

Hallie raised her arms to be picked up, and JenniLynn cuddled her close and kissed her apple-scented curls.

Once they'd helped tidy up, they went out onto the sidewalk and started their walk back to her car.

Lila pointed ahead of them. "Look. Mr. Grayson and Adam are walking up there. I have to go tell Adam I got the next book in the series we're both reading."

She ran toward them and Sasha followed, her shorter legs working double-time. She loved that Lila was an advanced reader for her age and was glad she and Adam had found something in common to talk about.

When Grayson heard them calling and turned around, he was already smiling, and her stomach did a flip-flop. She suddenly realized how much she'd missed him, and it had only been a couple of days since she'd seen him. There was no denying it. She had a huge crush on him.

She adjusted Hallie on her hip and continued their way.

"Good evening, Mayor Jenni."

When he called her by her title, it always made her smile. "Hello, Grayson."

"It's nice to see you again, Hallie." He held up his hand for a high-five.

Hallie just burrowed her face into JenniLynn's shoulder. As they walked along Central Avenue, her daughter remained on her hip, but the other three kids walked ahead of them. Lila held her little sister's hand but leaned to whisper to Adam. There was a moment of back and forth before they stopped and turned back to the adults.

"Can we eat at Castillo's?" they said in unison. "Please."

Sasha looked up at the two older kids with an accusatory glare—likely for being left out of the plan—but she must've decided it was to her advantage because she turned her smile their way and quickly added, "Please, Mommy."

"They're really good at this. How do they always set us up?" Grayson said to her under his breath.

JenniLynn chuckled. "I was thinking the same thing. But I am pretty hungry. I could really go for a taco salad. Want to come along?" She'd just asked him to dinner, but she was counting this as a group date.

"Absolutely." Grayson hadn't expected to see JenniLynn and her girls this evening, but he was glad. Until seeing her again, he hadn't truly let himself admit how much he'd been thinking of her. "Kids, we're going to eat at Castillo's."

"Yay," they chorused.

With a finger up in the air, he made a swirling motion. "About-face, soldiers."

Sasha perched her fists on her hips. "What about my face?"

He tried not to laugh as he bent to her level. "You have a very beautiful face. When I said 'about-face' it was a way of saying for you to stop, turn around and go the other direction. The restaurant is that way." He pointed over his shoulder.

"Oh, okay." Sasha looked up at JenniLynn. "Mommy, about-face."

"Yes, ma'am." JenniLynn made a show of turning around with Hallie still on her hip and marching a few steps. "Who's coming with us?"

The kids rushed past her and marched in a line, with Lila leading and Adam as the caboose.

Grayson came up beside her on the same side as Hallie. The toddler reached out one finger and poked his shoulder. "Is she telling me to walk on the other side?"

"No. I think it means she's warming up to you."

That was welcome news. "How was your day?" he asked JenniLynn.

"Very productive, but I'm still behind on filing paperwork."

He snapped his fingers. "That reminds me. I think I've found the perfect client to work in your office."

"Oh, good. Tell me about them. My temporary assistant is not going to work out long term."

"Her name is Monica Bailey. She's in her early twenties and very smart, but she's also very shy."

"If you think she is a good fit, I would love to meet her."

"Can I bring her by your office tomorrow?"

"Yes. That works for me."

"Morning or afternoon?" he asked.

"The morning will be busy for me, but shortly after lunch would be a perfect time."

"Mommy." Hallie patted her cheek. "Down."

She put her on her feet and took her tiny hand in hers. It slowed them but suddenly JenniLynn was no longer in a rush to get anywhere other than where she was in this moment.

"Kids," Grayson called to them, "don't get too far ahead of us, please."

He couldn't help but notice some of the looks they were getting from passersby. There was a reasonable amount of curiosity and, if he wasn't mistaken, a bit of speculation. Some of the glances were on the sly while other people outright gawked at them.

A woman he'd seen working at the grocery store looked at them and then whispered to the man beside her without even taking her eyes off them. He feared a rumor was going to start and he'd already been warned how gossip spread like wildfire in Tenacity. He had a strong feeling that JenniLynn would not like to be the topic of said gossip. She'd already been a victim of that.

If she was noticing the attention they were drawing, she wasn't saying anything, so he decided not to bring up the subject.

Soon all six of them were seated near the back of the Mexican restaurant. Hallie had surprisingly wanted to sit between him and JenniLynn, and he was happy she finally trusted him enough to let him near.

The other three kids sat on one side, and it was a bit cozy, but they were good about it and made it work.

They were almost finished eating when Sasha bounced in her seat. "Mommy, I gotta go potty."

"Me, too," Lila added.

JenniLynn turned to Grayson. "I'm going to take them to the restroom. Can you watch Hallie?"

"Of course."

No sooner had they walked away than a three-piece mariachi band started playing and moving around the small restaurant. The din of conversation, clink of silverware and hum of a blender at the bar became even more chaotic by the addition of the loud music.

Hallie's face screwed up and she shook her head of blonde curls. "No, no."

"Hallie, it's okay."

She clasped her hands over her ears and pulled at her curls.

"Your mommy will be back very soon."

She looked at him with frightened eyes and trembling lips, hitting him straight in his heart. Grayson picked her up from her booster seat and settled her on his lap, cradling one side of the little girl's head against his chest and gently cupping his palm over her ear to soften the noise. Murmuring that everything was going to be okay, he felt her relax in his arms.

"Dad," Adam said from across the table. "Is she okay?"

"She'll be just fine. It's just a little noisy in here."

"Oh, she doesn't like the noise. Just like Oscar," Adam said and then went back to eating his last few bites of his taco.

A hot prickly wave swept over him. Like his autistic nephew.

All the little moments once again added up to something he'd suspected for a while now. Her limited speech and lack of eye contact. Stimming activities like the way she always lined up her food, her toys and random pebbles on the ground. He'd watched her straighten things that were askew, and loud noises bothered her. He didn't know Hallie well enough to know anything for sure but…the signs were there.

With all they'd been through over the past year, how could he tell JenniLynn that he thought her youngest daughter was exhibiting signs of being on the autism spectrum?

JenniLynn came back from the bathroom with Lila and Sasha, and her brow furrowed. "Is she okay?" she asked above the din of noise.

"Dad helped her not freak out when it got loud," Adam said. "He's good at that."

Grayson smiled at her over the top of her toddler's head. "She's okay now."

"He sure is good at it." JenniLynn sat down and patted Hallie's back. "Thanks for this."

"No problem. She just needed a little reassurance and help to calm down. Is everyone ready to go?"

"I think we are." She reached out her arms for her toddler. "Thanks for making our dinner more fun."

"Anytime," he said.

She didn't need the added stress of his suspicions. Jenni-Lynn needed a supportive friend. He sighed. Maybe he was getting in too deep with someone who wouldn't be able to reciprocate his feelings. Feelings that were growing without him being able to stop them.

Chapter Eleven

Around one in the afternoon the following day, JenniLynn was making a cup of coffee when someone knocked on her office door. "Come in."

The door opened, and she was pleased to see Grayson's handsome face. A now-familiar sensation swirled through her belly.

"Good afternoon, Mayor Garrett," he said. "I would like for you to meet Monica Bailey." He gestured to the young woman stepping into the doorway beside him.

"Hello, Monica." She walked forward to greet them, but having been warned about the young woman's aversion to being touched, she didn't offer her hand. "I'm so glad you could come by today."

"I'm happy to meet you, Mayor Garrett," she said in a soft voice with a shy smile. Her straight, dark hair fell in a shiny curtain to the middle of her back. Her deep purple dress was professional yet still feminine, and her black ballerina flats had a row of tiny rhinestones across the toes. Sasha would want a pair if she saw them.

"Can I get coffee or something cold to drink for either of you?"

Monica replied quickly. "No, thank you, ma'am."

"I'll join you in a cup," Grayson said.

"Both of you please have a seat at the conference table." Since she already knew how Grayson drank his coffee, she didn't have to ask. She also brought a bottle of cold water for Monica just in case.

"Is it okay if Mr. Abernathy stays while we talk?" the young woman asked.

"Of course. It is him who has brought us together today." They spent a few minutes getting to know one another and then she asked the young woman some questions about her work experience and skills.

"When I talk to people on the phone, I'm able to, I guess you could say, not be so shy. So, I'm good at making calls."

JenniLynn smiled at her. "That will come in very handy." Monica was an impressive young lady, and she liked her very much. "What would you need from me? What kind of environment do you like to work in?"

Monica looked at Grayson, and he smiled at her. "It's okay. You can tell Mayor Garrett what things make you uncomfortable and what helps you."

"Well, I prefer a quiet space to work. I tried a job at a reception desk in a busy lobby once." She shook her head as if the memory was disturbing. "There was so much noise and activity that I had trouble focusing. It was also a huge open space, and I'm more a fan of cozy spaces."

JenniLynn nodded. "I can understand that. I like a calm workspace, too."

Monica rested her folded hands on the table. "I like music playing softly."

"What kind of music?"

"My favorite is country, and my second favorite is classical."

"I like both of those. You are also welcome to wear headphones if it helps you." They talked for a few more minutes. "When can you start working for me?" JenniLynn asked her.

Monica smiled at Grayson and then at her. "I can start tomorrow."

"Oh, good. Since you mentioned liking cozy spaces, I have an idea." JenniLynn pointed to a closed door. "Right through there is a tiny office. It's currently being used for storage, but I've been wanting to clean it out. If you like it, you can make it your own."

Monica clasped her hands together as if she'd been given a gift. "I actually love cleaning out closets and organizing. I can make that my first project, if you'd like?"

"I would love that. Open it and have a look, and then you can make a plan."

While Monica checked out what she'd signed up for, Grayson gave JenniLynn's shoulders a quick squeeze. "Thank you."

"For what?" she asked. "You are the one who brought me this wonderful young woman."

"For being you."

That made a warm glow fill her from the inside out. She walked with Monica and Grayson to the front doors of Town Hall. A few of the council members were gathered nearby and chatting after their lunch meeting. One of them was the man she always butted heads with.

"Monica, I'll see you in the morning."

"You sure will, Mayor Garrett. Thank you for this opportunity."

"I'm excited to work with you."

"I'll see you later, Mayor," Grayson said, with a secret grin hiding at one corner of his mouth.

She waved as they left but kept her lips zipped. When it came to Grayson, she was always so tempted to say something that ended up coming off as flirty. She didn't want anything to be overheard and misconstrued. Her life was crazy enough without adding that kind of gossip to her already full plate.

The last thing she needed was a rumor going around that the recently divorced mayor was hooking up with the town's new, rich rancher.

On her way back to her office, her least favorite councilman, Billy Riley, caught up to her and kept pace. "I heard that your new boyfriend is doing a lot to help out the town."

Her stomach clenched. Had she just jinxed herself? "I don't have a boyfriend. Who are you referring to?"

His grin flashed like a Got You sign. "Grayson Abernathy. The rancher who just left."

He was just doing this to get under her skin, and she wasn't going to let him. She stopped walking so he wouldn't follow her into her office. "Mr. Abernathy is in fact doing a lot to help our town. You are probably referring to him donating to the Dinosaur Center or perhaps the Jobs Corps program he is helping us implement."

"I've heard something about both."

"He is also a job coach, and he was here to introduce me to the young woman you saw. I just hired her as my secretary. Was there something else you needed? If not, I have a phone call I really need to return."

"No. Nothing urgent." Billy took a few steps backward, but his grin remained, and he didn't take his eyes from her. "Let me know when we can have lunch. Or dinner. You can fill me in on the Job Corps thing."

Was he flirting with her? Is that why he was probing about a boyfriend? She worked hard to hide her revulsion. "I'll let you know. Have a nice evening, Mr. Riley," she said and turned to briskly walk away. Did he really think the way he behaved was going to make her want to date him? He might be young and handsome, but something about him rubbed her the wrong way.

She paused after closing her office door and then leaned against it. A better question: Did his flirting mean that people thought it was now officially okay for her to date?

She pushed that thought aside and settled into her desk chair, but before she could get back to work, she received a text message. Grayson's picture of Adam with Moon and Star made her smile. A second message came through.

Are you up for a puppy playdate this evening? I can bring dinner and scope out your yard for a dog run.

She smiled as thoughts of Grayson wiped away the icky feeling she'd gotten from the councilman's surprising attention.

Sounds perfect. I have a roast in the crockpot so there's no need to bring food. I'll text you once we're home.

When JenniLynn got home from work, she didn't put on her usual yoga pants and a comfy T-shirt. Instead, she slipped on a pale blue cotton sundress that made her feel feminine and flirty. She didn't second-guess her wardrobe choice or scold herself for wanting to look pretty. In front of her full-length mirror, she swished her skirt then spun to make it flare.

"What are you doing, Mommy?" Sasha asked from her bedroom doorway.

She stopped and held out her hands, and her daughter ran forward to take them. "I'm just changing out of my work clothes." They spun a few more times, making her little girl giggle.

"You look pretty, Mommy."

"Thank you, sweetie."

"Where are you going?"

"Nowhere. But we have company coming." They walked from the bedroom hand in hand. "Moon and Star are coming over to play with Sandy and Sparky."

"Yay! Are Mr. Grayson and Adam coming, too?"

"Of course. The puppies are too little to come alone."

"Oh, yeah." Sasha giggled and ran off yelling to her sisters that company was coming.

Would there come a day when their dogs would run back and forth through their ranches to visit each house?

She allowed herself a moment to daydream about a future where they blended their families. Blended their lives into something new, where they could support one another through the challenges of day-to-day life.

"Mommy, Sasha accidentally knocked over Hallie's blocks, and she's upset."

"I'll be there in a minute." She pictured Grayson comforting her two-year-old like he'd done at the restaurant, and she smiled, but then she stopped in her tracks and frowned.

Was she just looking for someone to fill a supportive role in her life? She couldn't let her crush on Grayson lead to a rebound relationship or her kids getting hurt. The last thing she wanted to do was take advantage of his friendship. Not to mention, trusting in him too deeply could lead to another betrayal.

Go slow, JenniLynn.

Grayson put on his hat, locked his front door and went down the porch steps. "Adam, are you ready to go?" he called from beside his truck.

His son appeared from the backyard with a puppy cradled in each arm. "We're ready. Moon and Star are going to be so happy to see their mom and brother."

"No doubt." He opened his truck's back door, and Adam put the wiggly pups into the carrier on the floorboard and zipped it up. "Are you looking forward to hanging out with the girls?"

"Yep. But it would be kind of cool if Ms. JenniLynn had a son my age."

"That would be cool." He started the truck, and they set off for Coyote Creek Ranch.

"Dad, let's talk," his nine-year-old said with a serious face.

"Of course." Grayson turned down the radio. "What's on your mind?"

"When I'm not here, you're all alone."

"Does that worry you?"

He shrugged. "I always have someone with me, but you don't. And I don't want you to be lonely."

He reached across the center console and squeezed his son's shoulder. "You don't have to worry about me. I'm doing just fine."

"I think I might have a way to fix it."

"You do?"

"Yep. Maybe Ms. JenniLynn wants to be your new wife. It would be pretty cool to have sisters."

Grayson was momentarily speechless. "You'd be okay with me getting married again?"

"Mom is married again. I think that means you can be, too. Are you gonna ask Ms. JenniLynn to marry you?"

"Hold up, buddy. That's moving a little fast. We aren't even dating."

"You're not?"

"We're just friends."

For now. But the way he was starting to feel about her, he was willing to wait for her to be ready for more than friendship.

"Then you should probably only ask her to be your girl-friend for now."

He chuckled. "I'll keep that in mind."

"Good. I want you to be happy."

"I have the best son ever. I love you, kiddo."

"Love you, too, Dad."

When they got out of the truck at JenniLynn's house, he could hear them in the backyard.

"Dad, you can carry Star." Adam handed him the tan puppy.

They walked around the white farmhouse and went through a gate into the backyard. The three little girls were sitting in a sandbox. Their puppy was digging, and the mama dog was stretched out beside the box. Adam ran to join them, and Grayson put Star down to waddle after his little boy.

JenniLynn was sitting on a swing that was hanging from a large tree in the back corner of the fenced area. She looked so pretty in a blue sundress. Her blond hair was loose and blowing around her shoulders.

When she saw him smiling at her, she put her bare feet on the ground and stopped the swing. "Hi."

"Don't stop having fun on my account," he said as he walked toward her. "Hi, girls."

"Hi, Mr. Grayson," the older two said. Hallie waved a red shovel at him.

All four of the dogs excitedly greeted one another with happy yips.

JenniLynn slipped on a pair of flip-flops and stood.

"Want something to drink? I have lemonade and a few other adult choices if you would prefer."

"I'll have lemonade, please." He wished he could ask for a little extra sugar in the form of a kiss.

After she fetched his drink they walked around her backyard and discussed adding a doghouse and a few other features that would make it more suitable for their pets.

"While you're here, can you help me lift a couple of boxes into the attic?"

"Of course. Let's do it while the kids are entertained." He put his glass on the picnic table.

"Lila, please keep an eye on your sisters while Mr. Grayson helps me put boxes into the attic."

"Okay, Mommy."

He made eye contact with Adam, and his son gave him a thumbs up and a nod, indicating he would look out for the girls.

He followed JenniLynn inside, through her kitchen and into the living room. That's when his focus shifted from the house to the woman in front of him. Her hips swayed enough to make her skirt swing around her shapely calves, and he really wished he could get a look at her legs in a pair of shorts.

She stopped, and he was so focused on her that he bumped into her and grasped her hips to keep her from pitching forward.

Her breath caught, and she leaned back against his chest.

"Sorry," he said, but he didn't let go of her hips, and she didn't pull away.

She looked up over her shoulder. "What are you sorry for?"

"Almost knocking you down because I was…wasn't paying attention."

Her grin was knowing. "And what exactly *were* you paying attention to?"

"Um…" He took his eyes off her and realized they were in a closet, surrounded by her clothes and the scent of her perfume. A small cozy space where it felt like they were the only two people in the world.

Turning in his gentle grasp, she rested her hands on his biceps. "Being only friends with you is harder than I thought it would be."

"Yes, it is." He let his hands rise to her waist, and she pressed closer, threading her arms around his neck and daring his body not to react.

"Do you think it's possible for us to…" She hesitated to finish her thought.

"You don't have to hold back with me. Say whatever you're feeling."

"What if we take it nice and slow and don't make any promises?"

He brushed his thumb over her cheek. "Sweetheart, I want you so much, but I want you to be ready, and you don't need to make any promises to me."

It might kill him, slowly and painfully, but he would do what she suggested.

JenniLynn trembled in the best way possible. His hands felt so big and strong on her waist, their warmth seeping through her cotton dress. His scent wrapped around her. She hadn't felt this alive and sexy since…

She couldn't remember when.

JenniLynn was torn between her head and her heart. There was a voice inside her screaming to be careful, and another telling her not to turn away from this man. Why was she resisting when she didn't have to? What was she waiting on?

"I want…"

He tucked her hair behind her ear. "Tell me what you want, sweetheart."

"I want to kiss you again. Knowing full well that I'm not cheating on anyone. Knowing that I'm a single woman who is entitled to be happy and enjoy life."

"You deserve to enjoy every good thing life has to offer. And I'm happy to help in any way you need."

Her fingers teased up the back of his neck and into his hair. "That's really good to hear. Will you kiss me?" she whispered in his ear.

She'd swear he growled, and it delighted her. One of his big hands cradled the small of her back as the other roamed on a slow path up her spine. "I would love to kiss you."

JenniLynn shivered as his lips trailed soft kisses along her jaw to one corner of her mouth. His fingers glided into her hair, sending a shower of tingles throughout her body. And then he captured her mouth in a kiss that rocked her world, literally making her knees weak.

She reminded herself to go slowly, but all she could think about was how she felt in Grayson's strong, protective arms.

Chapter Twelve

JenniLynn's girls were all tucked in and dreaming, and she had pushed work aside in favor of a nice hot bath to relax her muscles. She turned off the water and shivered as she stepped into the mounds of rose-scented bubbles. She had learned not to leave her phone charging in another room while she was in the bath—lest Sasha make another call— and had it with her on the little wooden stool she sat on while bathing the girls.

Plus, she didn't want to miss what had become her nightly phone call with Grayson. Although trusting another man was hard for her, his patience, openness and willingness to listen were reassuring. Those were qualities her ex-husband did not possess.

Over the past week, she and Grayson hadn't seen one another every day, but they had talked on the phone each evening before bed. Sometimes she was already snuggled under the covers in the dark. Listening to his deep voice, she could almost pretend he was beside her. They shared their day's ups and downs, and funny moments with their kids. They told stories about their childhoods, and shared some of their wishes and fears.

In moments of weakness, JenniLynn allowed herself to daydream about a perfect blended family. Days of chaos and fun, smiles and tears, and love. And at night after the kids were put to bed, time alone to be adults together.

Earlier in the week, he'd brought cheeseburgers to her office at Town Hall, and they had a working lunch to discuss the Tenacity Jobs Corps. They had plenty of business owners signed on to be a part of the program and dates scheduled for a few weeknight bootcamps, along with an opening dinner celebration that would be held in the Tenacity Town Hall auditorium. The bootcamp was designed to provide guidance and training, and if all went well, it would also be a lot of fun for the participants.

When she did get to spend time with Grayson, for puppy playdates and joint family outings like hiking and fishing, they were occasionally able to steal a moment alone. Their kisses had become increasingly passionate, but they always stopped before things went too far. She could tell how hard it was for him, and she was so lucky that he cared enough to give her the time she needed before jumping too quickly into something serious.

Instead of waiting for Grayson to call, she reached over the side of the tub for her towel, dried her hands and picked up her phone. She had something to ask him that she hoped could lead to them having some time alone. It rang twice before he answered.

"Hello. Do I have the pleasure of speaking with Sasha or Tenacity's fine mayor?" he asked playfully.

She chuckled. "That's Mayor Jenni, to you."

"One never knows. What's up this evening?"

"I have a question. My girls are going to a summer day camp this Saturday, and there is enough space for Adam if you think he'd like to go. There will be food and crafts and flag football that I thought he might enjoy."

"That sounds fun. I'll ask him in the morning and let you

know, but I'm pretty sure he will want to go. What are you planning to do while the girls are at camp?"

"That remains to be seen." She was feeling confident, but there was still a natural sense of nerves tickling her belly. "If you don't already have plans, how do you feel about going on an adventure with me?"

"Sweetheart, I like the way you think."

His voice had deepened even more than normal, and it made her shiver. "Good."

"What would you like to do?"

"That's up for debate. But we can't really go too far because we will have to pick up the kids at four that afternoon." With her foot, she turned on the hot water to keep her bath from cooling.

"Do I hear water running?"

"Yes, sir, you sure do."

"Are you in the bathtub?"

This time his voice had gone up an octave, and she smiled to herself. "I might be."

He groaned. "Are there bubbles?"

Even though he couldn't see her, she scooped up a handful of iridescent suds and blew them into the air. "Tons."

He mumbled something she couldn't quite make out. "You're not playing fair, Mayor Jenni."

She splashed a little just to tease him. "Whatever do you mean?"

"You know exactly." He chuckled. "And I don't want you to stop."

They talked for a few more minutes. "I'm turning into a prune, and I need to get out of the water," she said.

"I'll see you tomorrow for our lunch meeting. What kind of food should I bring?"

"I would love a chicken tender salad from The Silver Spur Café."

"You got it. With extra ranch and no olives. Good night, sweetheart."

"Sweet dreams, Grayson."

"With the bubble bath image you've put in my mind, I'm sure they will be very sweet dreams."

JenniLynn's heart gave a little jump.

I think I'm almost ready to sleep with Grayson.

The next day at work, JenniLynn texted Grayson to tell him what an absolute treasure Monica was. She had cleaned out the little office and sorted and organized everything. Her desk in her cozy little space was meticulously neat. Jenni-Lynn always gave Monica the option to have her door open or closed, and more and more often she was leaving it open as they got to know one another. And as if fairies came in at night, there were no longer stacks of file folders and papers on the conference table.

JenniLynn rolled back her desk chair and stood to stretch. She wiggled her bare toes on the plush area rug she kept beneath her desk. It was one of those self-indulgent things that added a little needed pampering to her day. "Monica, did Barrett Deroy send over that signed agreement?"

"Yes, ma'am." The young woman stepped into the doorway of her office where they could see one another. "I've already printed it and put it into the appropriate Job Corps folder."

"That's wonderful. Thank you. We're really getting things marked off the list for these events."

"We should be ready ahead of schedule."

"Good. I feel better having a little wiggle room." She glanced at her grandmother's pendulum clock on top of the bookcase. She would have been so proud of her for becoming the mayor of Tenacity, and having the clock here made JenniLynn feel like she was watching over her. "Finally, it's lunchtime."

"I'm going to take my break now," Monica said.

"Okay. You can leave the door open to the hallway on your way out. I have a lunch meeting on the way." She bit the inside of her cheek to keep from grinning. Lunch *date* was a more accurate term. Since Adam was spending time with Grayson's cousin Sage, they would have some time alone.

"Can I bring anything back for you?" Monica asked.

"No, thank you. Enjoy your lunch."

Monica left the door ajar, and it was only a few minutes later that JenniLynn heard Grayson's voice in the hallway outside of her office. She also recognized the gravely smoker's voice of Tammy, one of the women who had worked at Town Hall for many years.

"You are becoming quite a fixture around here, Mr. Abernathy."

"There has been a lot of work to get done for the Tenacity Job Corps, so we fit in meetings when we can," he said.

"Oh, is that right?"

"It sure is. I want to do my part to help Tenacity be the best place it can be for every resident. Employers and employees."

"Well then, I better let you get to your lunch date. I mean meeting. Have a nice day."

"You, too."

JenniLynn could tell by the tone of Grayson's voice that he was annoyed with the busybody, and she didn't blame him. She was bothered by it, too.

When he stepped inside her office and closed the door

behind him, his expression was concerned. "Did you hear all that?"

"I sure did." She adjusted the window blinds so no one could see in.

He put two paper bags of food on the conference table and then leaned down for a quick kiss and rested his hands on her hips. "Does that probing question kind of thing happen often around here?"

"I think everyone is trying to figure out if I'm dating yet. There are probably bets about it going around town."

"Seriously?" he asked.

She sighed and rested her hands on his biceps because she liked the solid strength of him. "Well, I said it jokingly, but I'm not exactly sure. I had a weird conversation with one of the councilmen right after you and Monica were here for her interview."

"Weird how?" He seemed worried, and she put her arms around his neck.

"He was probing to see if you were my boyfriend. I thought it was because he wanted to go out with me, because when I said I didn't have a boyfriend, he said we should get together for lunch or dinner."

"Are you getting a meal with him?"

"I blew him off. He's always given me a playboy vibe I don't go for. But speaking of meals…" She went up onto her toes and pressed a gentle but lingering kiss to his lips, ending with a nip of her teeth. "I'm starving. Let's eat."

When she turned to open the to-go bags, he chuckled and stepped up behind her and kissed her cheek. "For a second there, I thought you were going to have me for lunch."

"As tempting as that is, that's not going to happen in the mayor's office on my watch."

"I find your morals and values very sexy, Mayor Jenni."

"Good. But… I won't say I haven't been thinking about things happening *away* from work more and more." She blushed and ducked her head. "I can see us moving our relationship to the next level sometime soon."

"What does the next level mean to you?"

"Sharing a bed."

Those were words that Grayson had been waiting to hear, but he wanted her to be able to look him in the eyes when she was truly ready to be his lover. Grayson tipped up her chin. "You are in the driver's seat, sweetheart. And I'm happy to go along for the ride until you say we're there."

"How did I get so lucky?"

"I think we are both lucky. I wanted to bring you flowers, but that would surely start a rumor, so…" From the second paper sack, he pulled out a bouquet of colorful ink pens tied together with a big pink bow.

She laughed and hugged his gift to her chest. "It's perfect. I love them, and they will last a lot longer than flowers."

They spread out the food, got drinks from the mini-fridge and started eating.

"Grayson, have you noticed people staring at us when we're out in public together?"

He had been worried that she was going to start pulling away if people kept interfering in their business. He hated that she had to worry about stuff like this and had been hoping she hadn't noticed. "People always stare at me. It's just part of my charm."

She smiled, which had been his goal. "It's the two of us together that seems to be drawing attention and some talk around town."

"I think it's only natural. People are curious, and you are a public figure."

"That's what I'm worried about. My public image."

"I'll remind you again, we are not doing anything wrong."

"I know. I just hate gossip and rumors. I want residents to focus on my professional contributions to the community, not my personal life or dating habits." She added another drizzle of ranch dressing to her salad.

"Haven't lots of the people in Tenacity known you all your life?"

"Yes. I know most people want the best for me, but there are others who no doubt hope for a bit of juicy gossip." She put down her fork and met his gaze. "So, when we have our kid-free day on Saturday, maybe we should choose an activity that is out of the public eye."

"What about that hiking trail that was too rigorous for the kids? We could pack a lunch and try it out."

"That sounds perfect. It's close enough to town but a place we likely won't see anyone we know."

He was glad she liked the idea, because he knew if they spent all of their kid-free time at one of their houses, they might end up in bed before she was truly ready.

On Saturday morning, Grayson was looking forward to spending some quality time alone with JenniLynn while all four of the kids were at the summer day camp.

The older two kids were feeding and walking the dogs while JenniLynn got Hallie ready, and he sat in her living room to catch a bit of the baseball game on TV.

Sasha skipped into the room and stopped in front of his chair with her hands on her hips. One of her braids was still tightly secured, but the other was loose and wild around her rosy cheek. Almost as if it had been purposely mussed. The upward curve of her mouth and the twinkle in her eyes was yet another clue that she was up to something.

"Can I help you?" he asked with a straight face.

"Can you braid hair?" she asked, with a tilt of her head that was just like one of her mom's expressions.

"Yes, I sure can." Thanks to his sisters, he could accept this little one's challenge. "Would you like me to fix your hair?"

She cocked her head as if making up her mind if he was serious or not. "Yes. Please," she added in a rush, as if she no doubt remembered the discussion about manners that they'd all had while having dinner together a few nights ago.

"Do you have a brush and a rubber band?"

"Yep." She held up both hands and with one she produced a purple hairbrush with a unicorn painted on the back and a tiny rubber band on one finger of her other hand.

He took the items, and she turned to the side. He started brushing out the tangles as gently as he could. "Did a bat fly into your hair and have a dance party?"

She giggled. "No. Not a bat. It was a… I think my baby sister did it."

"Did she now? Are you trying to get Hallie into trouble?"

She tilted her head to look up at him. "Maybe it was just the wind. Nobody needs to be in trouble."

"Oh, that's good to hear."

While he divided her hair into three sections and began braiding, she chattered away about the backyard squirrels and getting in trouble for sneaking a cookie.

JenniLynn walked into the living room and stopped short, staring at him as if she was shocked, and he suddenly worried that he'd stepped over some line.

Chapter Thirteen

A slow smile spread across her face, and she changed directions, making her way over to them. "You are full of surprises, Grayson Abernathy."

JenniLynn sat on the sofa beside him as he put a rubber band on the end of her daughter's braid. Her ex had refused to even consider learning how to do the girls' hair, and this man was a pro at it.

"Mommy, Mr. Grayson can braid hair. Can you believe it?" She leaned in and quickly kissed his cheek and then bounced away while singing a song.

"Wow," JenniLynn said as she watched her daughter skip down the hallway. Her difficult middle child really liked Grayson. It was suspiciously like she was giving him a tryout to see if he could make the team.

A flicker of worry burned in JenniLynn's stomach. She was just learning to be self-sufficient. Were her children getting too attached and starting to rely on Grayson? If things ended badly between them, how would she pick up the pieces a second time? She'd put her trust in the wrong man with Rob. But Grayson was...different. Wasn't he?

"Did I do something wrong?" Grayson asked.

She cut her gaze to him. "No. What makes you think that?"

"It was just the way you reacted when you first came into the room, and now you've gone quiet. I thought maybe I'd overstepped by doing her hair."

"I was just surprised. Not mad. I think it's sweet that you helped her and didn't just tell her to go find me. Who taught you to braid?"

"My sisters, Amanda and Evie. We used to braid the horses' tails and manes. I get the feeling that it's a surprise that I know how?"

"Their dad can't do it." She worried her lip with her teeth, debating how much she should say. The warmth of his hand on top of hers felt like an offer to listen without judgement and she took the opportunity, but she lowered her voice. "Rob wouldn't even try to learn how. There are a lot of parenting skills he is lacking. We agreed to him having five visits per month with the girls, but since he's living with his parents in Bronco, they've dwindled to just a couple of times a month. He always has an excuse."

Grayson's jaw muscles flexed and stood out in sharp relief, as if he was clenching his teeth to keep from saying the wrong thing. She wouldn't have been surprised to hear a growl, but he only stared toward the windows.

Even though Grayson was divorced, she didn't believe he was the kind of man who so easily walked away—like her ex had done. But the fear of her kids getting too close to someone new and then getting hurt was one of the main things holding her back.

He exhaled and then turned to her with a smile. "I marvel at your strength, sweetheart."

"Thanks. That's nice to hear." She laced her fingers with his and felt him relax even more. He always made her feel so…seen. And empowered. "So, tell me, cowboy. Did Sasha ask you to do her hair or did you offer?"

"She came to me with one braid in complete disarray, a hairbrush and a rubber band. It felt a little bit like a challenge."

"I think Sasha was testing you."

"I got the same feeling. Why do you think she's doing it?"

The question made JenniLynn's heart jump uncomfortably. She had a feeling it was because her little girl might want a new daddy after all, but she couldn't say that to Grayson. The idea frightened her too much. Sasha was getting attached to both him and Adam, and she needed to talk to all three of her girls about their expectations.

"Sasha's too-smart-for-her-age mind sometimes works in mysterious ways, and it could be so many reasons. I should probably ask her about it before I speculate."

"That's a good idea. I like your parenting style." His thumb brushed softly over her knuckles. "She told me she got in trouble for sneaking cookies last night."

"Sasha is honest, sometimes even at her own expense."

He chuckled. "At one point she blamed her messed-up hair on her baby sister, but when I asked if Hallie should be in trouble, she blamed it on the wind."

"She is the sweetest little whirlwind ever." She rested her head on his shoulder, and he put his arm around her. "But I fear she's going to be the troublemaker who always gets caught because she's too honest and gives herself away. I better work on teaching her to not get into trouble in the first place."

"Your girls are proof that you're a great mom." He lifted their linked hands and kissed the back of hers. "I look forward to watching them grow up."

JenniLynn felt Grayson tense a split second after the words left his lips. Freezing as if he'd surprised himself.

She tipped her head to look at him, and when their gazes

locked, they both smiled. She didn't ask him to explain his comment. Whether he meant he'd see her girls grow up because they were neighbors in the same small town or because of something deeper.

"We better get these kids to day camp before they are late. Time is wasting." She jumped up and pulled him to his feet.

"I couldn't agree more."

Her heart was so full these last few weeks, and she was starting to wonder… Could there be something lasting between them?

After the four kids were dropped off at day camp, the two of them drove to the trailhead and parked. They each carried a backpack and set off on the easy portion of the trail. A pleasant breeze rustled the leaves, and the sound of nature mixed with the earthy scents was such a calming combination. Until she remembered she hadn't taken her allergy medication.

She reached into the front pocket of her new khaki shorts, but the pocket was empty. "Oh, snapdragon."

He chuckled. "Sorry to laugh. That's a new one. Did you lose something?"

"No. I put my allergy pill in the pocket of my denim shorts, but then I changed into these."

He stopped walking. "Do we need to go home to get it?"

"I'll be fine. I'll take it when I get home." She took hold of his hand, and they continued.

Grayson had swapped out his cowboy attire for cargo pants, hiking boots and a baseball cap. It made her think about what he might have looked like in his younger college days. "Adam told me you played football in college."

"I did. Gosh, that seems like a lifetime ago."

She studied his profile. "The years don't show on your

face. I would've sworn you were around thirty-four like me. I was surprised when you said you were forty."

He grinned as if her compliment embarrassed him. "When's the last time you had your vision checked?"

"Last month."

"Did they say you have stars in your pretty blue eyes?"

"No, but if I went today, they might." Her answer brought a big smile to his face.

They moved closer together as a couple of teenaged boys ran by, laughing and teasing one another about a girl. It made her think of the teens joining the Job's Corps program. "Are you okay with me putting Monica in charge of food and activities for the picnic we're planning for the young clients?"

"Absolutely. She'll be very sensitive to everyone's needs. It's a testament to our program to see you and Monica working so well together."

At the junction of the more difficult trail, she veered off the flat section they'd walked with the kids to go up the challenging portion with the beautiful overlook at the top. "Better keep up with me, cowboy. Unless you want to lead the way?" she asked over her shoulder.

"Nope. I'm very happy walking behind you."

"Should I ask why?"

"Because if I'm in front of you, I can't see how pretty you are."

"From your current vantage point, which part of me are you looking at?"

"The whole pretty package, sweetheart. From your shiny hair to the pink and gray hiking boots that look so cute on your little feet."

She stopped and turned to Grayson, her perch on a rock putting her a head above him. She spread her fingers on his shoulders, loving the stable support he offered. In this quiet moment in the middle of the forest, he felt as stable as the massive trees surrounding them. "You really are the sweetest charmer I've ever known."

Wrapping his arms around her waist, he pulled her closer. "You bring it out in me, sweetheart."

"Do I make you feel playful?" That was something she hadn't had in the last few years of her marriage—if ever.

"Yes, ma'am. Playful and adventurous and excited about the future."

She gently held his cheeks and kissed him softly, trying to tell him without words how much his support meant to her. "I'm really glad we're getting to know one another. You're helping me find a path through to the other side of... I'm not sure how to put it into words."

"Is it that I'm encouraging you?" He took both of her hands and raised her outstretched arms high into the air above his own head. "That I want you to soar like a bird to whatever heights you want to reach?"

She smiled at him through a sheen of tears. "Yes."

JenniLynn's voice stopped working as her major crush on this handsome man became so much more. Real feelings bloomed in a rush, and she once again wrapped her arms around him and hugged him close.

I'm falling in love. The thought made warmth bloom in the center of her chest.

He held her so tenderly yet fiercely at the same time. "We're both starting new chapters of our lives, and I believe this is the start of something amazing."

JenniLynn pressed her cheek to his. "I couldn't have said it better myself."

"And if you ever feel scared or rushed, say the word, sweetheart."

She shivered as his whispered words feathered against her skin. Was Grayson Abernathy a man she could count on long-term, or one of those too-good-to-be-true things that could bring you to your knees?

Grayson couldn't stop smiling as he climbed the trail behind her. JenniLynn had not seemed shocked or upset by his earlier comment about watching her girls grow up. He hadn't planned to say it. It had just naturally come out. What did it mean? Was she thinking along the same lines he was?

He took a moment to consider what his comment meant to him. Did he want JenniLynn and her three little girls to be a permanent part of his life?

As the answer formed in his mind, a tingly sensation made his pulse jump. Yes. He did. He could see their kids growing up as siblings. He could see them building a beautiful, full life together.

Whoa, dude. Slow down. There's no rush.

He forced himself to take a breath. He'd jumped into a relationship too soon once before, and what he had with JenniLynn was too special to rush.

As she stopped above him to tie her shoe, sunbeams made her hair sparkle. A smile overtook his face. Sasha would love that he'd incorporated the word *sparkle* into his vocabulary.

"What are you smiling about?" she asked.

"I was just noticing how the sunlight is making your hair sparkly and thinking how much Sasha would like that description."

"She certainly would. I love that you know that little fact." She took a couple of steps then stopped with one foot on a large tree root. "I just remembered one of my grandmother's sayings. 'A man who pays attention to the little things is a gem worth keeping.'"

"I think I would've liked your grandmother," he said.

"She would've adored you."

When JenniLynn flashed a dazzling smile that outshone the sunbeams, he fell all the way in love.

So much for slowing things down.

At the top of the trail, they were both breathing heavily, but the scene before them was fit for a postcard. They looked out over a valley in varying shades of green with a river snaking through the center.

"You were right. This view is worth the climb."

"I'm glad you think so. Let's sit right over there and eat." On a flat-topped boulder, they sat side-by-side and spread out their lunch.

He wondered if Adam could make this climb. He'd love to share this view with his son… Before he went back to his mom's house.

An unwelcome stab of pain struck his chest. That dreaded reality was always hovering like a dark cloud ready to send a lightning strike, but because he was with JenniLynn, he didn't feel the need to censor his feelings as closely as he did with most people. "Adam told me he's worried that I'm lonely when he's not around."

"Aww, you have the sweetest son. You and his mom have raised him right."

"We were driving over to your place for our first puppy playdate." Grayson drew up his leg and braced his arm on his knee. "Now remember, these ideas and thoughts are coming from a little kid."

"Oh, this should be good," she said. "Tell me what he said."

"He suggested you could be my wife so I wouldn't be lonely." Her eyes widened, accompanied by a soft gasp, but he continued before she could get the wrong idea. "When I told him we weren't even dating, he was surprised. He thought you were my girlfriend."

"Grayson, do you think everyone who sees us together thinks we're a couple?"

"I don't think so." He hadn't meant to upset her.

"You know what?" She waved a hand through the air as if to wipe the thought aside. "I'm not going to even worry about that today. Let's just enjoy the moment we're in."

"Best plan I've heard in a long time."

A couple of hours later, they were back on the easy, level section of the trail and almost to their car when voices could be heard coming toward them.

"Oh, no," JenniLynn whispered and dropped his hand. "I know those voices."

An old couple from Tenacity came around a curve in the flat section of the trail, and when they saw JenniLynn and Grayson, their eyes lit up, no doubt with the prospect of a bit of juicy gossip.

"Fancy seeing you two. Together. Again," said Mrs. Phillips.

JenniLynn tensed. Of course, the couple weren't just going to say hello and mind their own business.

"When did we see them together?" the old man asked his wife in a voice a little too loud, as if he didn't have his hearing aids turned on.

"We saw them at Castillo's."

He held up a weathered hand and shook his pointer finger in the air. "Oh, yeah. With all the little kids packed into the booth."

He and JenniLynn shared a look. "Our kids are all at the same day camp. Since Mr. Abernathy is new to the area,

I'm showing him some of what our area of Montana has to offer."

"Didn't we see you together at the grocery store, too?" the old man asked Grayson.

"I don't think so, sir. But I have seen you at Tenacity Feed and Seed."

"Oh, yeah. You drive the fancy silver double-cab truck."

"That's right."

"It was nice to see you both," JenniLynn said. "I need to get back to town to pick up the girls. Have a nice walk," she said over her shoulder.

"Be careful being seen together too often," Mrs. Phillips called after them. "People might talk."

"Like you," Grayson mumbled under his breath as soon as they were out of earshot. "I'm sorry about that, Jenni-Lynn. Are you freaked out?"

She smiled at him, but it seemed strained. "I'm not going to let two nosey people ruin my day."

Since they still had time before getting the kids, they went back to his house where all four of the dogs were hanging out together in his backyard run. He brought her a cold bottle of her favorite sparkling water and sat beside her on the couch.

"I think Adam is right," she said.

He waited for her to say more, but she seemed deep in thought. "What is he right about?"

"I think I have been your secret girlfriend."

"Why did you keep it a secret from me?" he asked with a smile.

"I'm just figuring it out." She laughed and hooked her leg over his knee. "Am I freaking you out?"

"No, ma'am." The smooth skin of her thigh was warm

under his palm, and he wanted so much to explore the rest of her. "I would love for you to officially be my secret girl-friend."

She kissed his jaw. "Grayson, you are giving me more than I deserve. Your patience is amazing."

"You deserve it all. When you are ready to be my lover, all you have to do is say you're ready." He watched her expression shift into several expressions he couldn't name as she seemed to wrestle with a decision.

"I promise you'll be the first to know. How do you feel about making out on your couch?"

"You read my mind, Mayor." With all of their clothing in the way, he kissed her until they were both boneless.

JenniLynn looked over his shoulder and gasped. "Grayson, it's 3:45! We have to pick up the kids."

"Oh, fudgesicle," he said, and made her laugh as they raced out the door.

Chapter Fourteen

"Should we have driven separately to pick up the kids?" Grayson asked JenniLynn as she pulled into the pick-up line of cars at the church.

"We probably should have." She sighed. "It's too late now." She inhaled a long slow breath as if coming to a decision. "Since news of us hanging out is already spreading, maybe we should just let things happen naturally. Not outright announce it or anything like that."

He could see the concern in her eyes. "If we just act totally casual with no public affection, there will be nothing for them to talk about."

She looked at him as if that was wishful thinking. "Here's hoping," she said as she moved up in the line of cars.

As they made it to the front of the line, there was no lack of staring, and he once again wished they'd come separately so she wouldn't get spooked by this much attention so soon after their decision to officially date. But they'd been in such a rush—and he'd been on such a high from her kisses—he hadn't been thinking clearly.

They both got out to help get the kids into her SUV and buckled booster seats.

"Was it fun?" Grayson asked them as they pulled away from the curb.

"I got to play on a flag football team, and I met lots of guys," Adam said.

"That's great."

"I didn't play football," Lila said. "I was too busy doing other stuff. Hallie stayed with Courtney most of the day."

On the drive to Ambling Hills, everyone except Hallie wanted to tell them about their day. The toddler held a stuffed lion against one ear and a penguin against the other and tapped her toes together until she fell asleep. Grayson couldn't help but notice her self-soothing behavior and wondered if noise-canceling headphones might help her.

"Dad, which house are we having dinner at?" Adam asked.

"Well, all the dogs are at our house." Grayson looked at JenniLynn before he said more.

"I'll tell you what," she said. "When we get there, I'll have a look in your pantry and refrigerator and if there is what we need, I'll give you a cooking lesson."

"What if we don't have the right stuff?" Adam asked her.

"I bet I can figure something out."

"Can we all help?" Lila asked. "I like making up new recipes."

"Sure, sweetie. Anyone who wants to can help."

Grayson smiled at her from the passenger seat. "Good thing I have a big kitchen."

Later, with all four kids sitting on stools on one side of his kitchen island, they prepared to make dinner. Four sweet faces looked to JenniLynn to feed them something yummy.

Grayson opened the pantry and then stood back to offer her free reign. "Let's see what magic you can come up with."

She studied the shelves for a moment and then grabbed a bag of spaghetti and put it on the island. JenniLynn opened the side-by-side refrigerator and freezer, talking to them as she got things out. "Perfect. Half a rotisserie chicken, frozen peas and carrots, butter and the rest of the white wine I left over here." She braced her hands on the countertop with the assortment of ingredients in front of them. "Okay, everyone. What can we do with all this?"

"Eat it," Sasha said proudly. "Is that the right answer?"

Adam stifled a laugh behind his hand.

"Sounds right to me," Grayson said.

Lila picked up the stick of butter. "Mommy, make your wine sauce and then we can mix everything together."

JenniLynn smiled at her oldest. "Excellent idea, sweetie. We can boil the pasta, make a white wine butter sauce and toss it with the diced chicken and vegetables."

Adam braced his arms on the countertop. "That sounds fancy and hard to do."

"It's so much easier than you think." She started assigning jobs.

Grayson was in charge of the sharp knife and carved up the roasted chicken, while the kids poured the frozen peas and carrots into a steamer basket and filled the pasta pot. They decided they should watch a cartoon until it was time to mix everything together.

"Come over here, cowboy," JenniLynn said with a crook of her finger. "I'm going to teach you how to make a simple white wine butter sauce."

Eager to learn whatever she wanted to teach him, he moved in beside her.

Leftover rotisserie chicken became something that seemed so much fancier, and it was the first big family meal at his dining room table.

As the girls drove away after dinner, Adam grinned up at him. "She's your girlfriend now, isn't she?"

He returned his son's smile and couldn't bring himself to lie to him. "Yes, she is. But we're keeping it quiet for now. She hasn't told her girls yet, so we need to keep it between you and me."

"And Ms. JenniLynn," Adam pointed out.

"That's right." He put his hand on his son's small back, guided him inside the house and over to the sofa where they could sit and talk. "Lila, Sasha and Hallie have had a rough year, and their dad hasn't been gone that long."

As the words left his mouth, a thought popped into Grayson's head. Was JenniLynn worried that people would suspect there had been something romantic between them before her divorce was final? It wasn't true, but that wouldn't stop a rumor.

"So, all the girls are still sad about their dad?" Adam asked.

"Yes. We need to let Ms. JenniLynn tell them about us when she thinks they are ready. Can you do that?"

"I know how to keep a secret, Dad."

"Thanks, buddy." He hated the idea of asking his son to keep secrets. "I'll let you know when it's okay to share the news."

"When will that be?"

He had the same question. "I'm not sure, son."

JenniLynn was not having a great day at work, and she was more grateful for Monica than ever. She'd awakened with a headache that had hung around all morning, even after caffeine and aspirin and an allergy pill.

While walking around Town Hall, she didn't think it was her imagination that everyone was staring at her as if she'd forgotten some important piece of clothing. With a quick check, she assured herself that her outfit was complete and her shoes matched.

"Mayor Garrett," Tammy said in her gravely smoker's voice. "When does your husband's trial start?"

Her stomach tightened uncomfortably. "My *ex-husband's* trial starts in a few weeks."

"Sorry. I meant to say ex-husband. How are your children handling all that?"

"We're all doing the best we can." The other woman's cellphone rang, and JenniLynn jumped on the chance to get away. "I'll let you get that."

Why couldn't people mind their own damn business? She decided to go back to her office before someone annoyed her enough that she snapped at them. She'd been working so hard to make up for what her husband had done to the whole town, and her girls hearing gossip was one of her biggest fears. Tonight, she should talk to all three of them and…

Do what? Try to explain things that were beyond their years? JenniLynn sighed and grabbed a bottle of sparkling water from the small refrigerator. She was worried that she was getting sick because she hadn't taken her medication before their hike, and now her headache and itchy nose and throat were developing into something more.

Monica brought her soup for lunch. She would have called Grayson, but he and Adam were having a father and son day in Bronco, and she wasn't about to interrupt their precious time together.

With her eyes aching, she leaned back in her desk chair and closed them, wishing she had a couch in her office.

"Mayor Garrett," Monica said. "Why don't you just go home and get some rest. I can handle things here for the rest of the day."

JenniLynn opened her eyes and smiled at the sweet young woman standing in front of her desk. "Maybe I should."

She felt ill, people were being gossipy and annoying, and she wasn't getting anything productive done. She really hoped none of her girls were feeling bad, but she hadn't received a call from daycare, so that was a good sign. Besides, she was pretty sure this stemmed from her allergies. "I think I'll also call my doctor before his office closes."

"That's a good idea."

After going over a few things with Monica, she grabbed her purse and laptop bag and left. She picked up the girls, checked that everyone was feeling okay and they were finally on their way home.

"Mommy, don't forget to stop at the feedstore. We need chicken food," Lila reminded her.

"Oh, that's right. I totally forgot." The sun flashed in her eyes, and she grimaced. All she wanted to do was go home, make something simple for dinner and go to bed early, but she couldn't quit being a single, working mom yet. She pulled into the parking lot of Tenacity Feed and Seed and parked in front of the entrance.

"You girls stay in the car, please. I'm just going to run inside to the front counter and tell them what to put on our account, and then we'll drive around to the side so they can load it."

"I'll read a story to them," Lila offered.

"Thank you, sweetie."

Before she could reach the front door, it opened and Timothy, a guy she'd known since high school, came out. "Hey, JenniLynn. How's it going?"

"It's going pretty well." She glanced over her shoulder at the girls, who were all looking at the book Lila held up.

"I heard you're dating now. So, I was wondering, would you like to go dancing sometime?"

That snapped her attention right back to him. "Who told you I was dating?"

"I heard it around town."

She sighed and rubbed her cheek. "I'm sorry, but you got inaccurate information."

Timothy looked truly horrified. "Oh, JenniLynn, I'm so sorry. I shouldn't have said anything. I should have known better than to listen to gossip."

"It's alright." She forced a smile. "I have nothing against dancing with you. I'm just not dating right now." That felt like a lie, and she glanced at her feet.

"Forgive my boldness," he said.

"No apology needed." This time her smile was real. "Have a nice evening and save a dance for me at the next town event."

"I sure will." Timothy waved to her girls on the way to his truck.

The young woman at the register asked her if she was going to go out with Timothy and kept going on and on about how cute he was. JenniLynn once again stated that she was not dating.

By the time they got home, her whole body was aching. She received a return call from her doctor, and since he'd been familiar with her allergies and symptoms for so many years, he called in a prescription. Thank goodness their small-town pharmacy delivered, because she was too tired to go back into town for it today.

"Are you okay, Mommy?" Sasha asked.

"I'm not feeling so good tonight. Are all of you still feeling okay?"

Sasha stretched out across the back of the couch then

rolled onto the seat cushions. "You already asked us that when you picked us up at daycare."

"I just want to make sure. If anyone starts feeling sick, let me know, please."

Lila and Sasha assured her they were fine, and Hallie didn't answer, but she appeared okay. "We're having frozen pizza for dinner and watching a movie after an early bath. Mommy needs some extra rest tonight."

"We'll take care of you." Sasha kissed the top of her head like JenniLynn often did to them.

"Thank you, sweet girl. Why don't you go pick out your pajamas and a pair for Hallie while I preheat the oven. Then I'll come run your bath."

An hour later, her crew was fed, bathed and cozied up on beanbags in front of the television. Sandy was in her favorite spot beside Hallie, and the puppy was cuddled between Sasha and Lila. She curled up on the couch with a mug of hot tea and a pill.

The worse she felt, the more her anxiety rose. Her mind jumped among a whole list of worries. Things like what needed to be done at work, the gossip about her love life, Rob's upcoming trial and guilt over letting the television babysit her girls. She should be using this time to talk to them about…so many things. But how did you talk to young children about something as complicated as town gossip or a new relationship? And she still hadn't asked Sasha more about why she asked him to braid her hair. She wasn't sure where or how to start the conversation.

Rather than run the risk of saying the wrong thing because she was emotional, she sipped her herbal tea and silently admired her girls.

When her phone rang, JenniLynn slipped into her bedroom to answer Grayson's call.

"Hello," she said, and then swallowed a sudden lump in her throat.

"Hi, sweetheart."

"Are you home from Bronco?"

"We got back about an hour ago. Adam is in the shower and then we are going to have popcorn and watch the third movie of a sci-fi series."

"How was your big day out?"

"It was great. Adam had a lot of fun. Well, we both did. What about you?"

She sat on the edge of her bed. "Not as great as yours."

"What happened, sweetheart?"

She could hear the worry in his voice, but she decided not to tell him she was sick. She didn't want to interrupt their father and son time.

"Nothing terrible. I've just had a headache since I woke up, and then I had to deal with gossip."

"Oh, no. Tell me."

She told him about the stares that seemed to follow her everywhere, and her gossip-induced encounters at Town Hall and at the feedstore.

"I can hear it in your voice," he said. "You want to slow down, don't you?"

He said what she had not been able to admit to herself. "With Rob's trial coming up soon, I think his ballot tampering and our divorce are back on everyone's mind. I don't want to draw more attention than necessary by being seen together. The timing is just…bad. I have to protect my girls."

Not to mention her own heart.

He was quiet, and she knew this was not what he wanted to hear. It wasn't what she wanted to say. Her eyes and throat burned as she held back the tears. Being a mom to her precious children and being the town's mayor had to come before her dating life.

"JenniLynn, what do you want to do?" he asked.

"I've been telling people that I'm not dating anyone, but that's a lie. I feel like we've been flaunting it in their faces."

"How about no more public appearances?" he suggested.

She sighed, hating this interruption to their relationship so much. "I think for now, that's best. It's just bad timing."

Physically, she was feeling lousier by the second, and emotionally, she felt a messy mix of guilt and fear. She felt completely overwhelmed by work and motherhood and trying to be everything to everyone. Working-mother guilt was eating at her. Basically, she wanted to crawl into bed and cry, but she had little girls in the other room who needed her to be strong.

"Grayson, maybe I'm rushing myself."

He cleared his throat. "You know where I stand on things. I don't want you to do anything you aren't comfortable with or aren't ready for. I'll wait for you to… Well, you know where to find me when you need me."

"One of these days soon, you're going to get tired of me being afraid." She didn't like the long pause she heard on the line.

"Not today," he finally said, but the usual joy in his voice had dimmed. "I need to go check on Adam."

"You two have fun."

"Goodnight, JenniLynn."

The phone line went dead, and she closed herself in the bathroom and let the tears fall.

Chapter Fifteen

Grayson's phone rang and pulled him from a deep sleep. He blinked enough to see that the sun was barely coming up and was still half asleep when he answered JenniLynn's call.

"Sweetheart, are you okay?"

"I'm okay," Sasha said.

He flopped back onto his pillow and smiled. The little munchkin had gotten hold of her mom's phone again.

"I'm okay, too." He heard Lila's voice chime in. "But Mommy is sick."

That woke him all the way, and he sat up. "What's wrong with her?"

"She's all sweaty and moaning and stuff," Sasha said.

"Did she ask you to call me?"

"No," Lila replied, "but Sasha and I talked about it and decided we needed help from a grownup. We can't even use the oven by ourselves to make get-well cookies."

"Is Hallie okay?"

"She's still sleeping."

"I'm going to wake Adam up, get dressed and come over to your house."

"Thank you, Mr. Grayson," they said in tandem.

"Call me back if you need to." With his anxiety in full go mode, he pulled on yesterday's jeans and grabbed a clean shirt. He should've known last night that something more than gossip was going on with her sudden change of attitude about their relationship.

He went down the hall to wake Adam. "Son, I need you to wake up and put some clothes on, please."

He lifted his head. His hair was standing on end and only one eye was open. "What's wrong?"

"Sasha and Lila called and said their mom is sick. So, we're going over there to check on her."

Adam was already out of bed and reaching for clothes. "I'll meet you at the front door, Dad."

"I'll put on my boots and grab the puppies. Don't forget to brush your teeth."

They were there in ten minutes, but it felt like forever. If he could've driven from the back of his property onto hers, it would've only been five minutes. He was going to talk to Mr. Smith about buying his farm or at least asking for permission to add a gate and access through to Jenni-Lynn's property.

The girls let him into the house, and the mama dog went outside with Sparky for a potty break. He put the carrier with Moon and Star on the kitchen floor.

Sasha threw her little arms around his legs. "You came."

"Of course I did, honey." He patted her back. "I'll go check on your mommy. Adam, why don't you get the puppies out and hang out in the family room with the girls."

"Okay, Dad."

He moved quietly into JenniLynn's bedroom and sat on the edge of her bed. His shoulders relaxed for the first time since Sasha's wake-up call. JenniLynn was breathing in a nice even rhythm, and even though there were dark circles under her eyes, she was one of the most beautiful sights he'd ever seen. He stroked her damp brow, but she didn't feel feverish.

She opened her eyes and blinked a few times. "Grayson? What are you doing here?"

"The girls called me. They were worried about you."

"Oh, no." She sat up and then immediately pressed one hand against the side of her head. "The girls."

"Everyone is fine. Hallie isn't even awake, yet." Her hair was mussed, and her nose was red, but he was so relieved that she was okay.

Scooting back, she leaned against the pink padded headboard. "I'm sorry they called and worried you."

"I'm not. I'm going to call Monica and tell her you aren't coming to work today, and then I'm going to take care of you and the girls."

"They can go to daycare," she said.

This was his chance to show her how different he was from her ex-husband. Taking care of four kids and her would be no problem. "Adam would love their company for the day, and I don't mind at all. It will be fun."

"Oh, Grayson." She sniffed and pulled a tissue from the box on her nightstand, then dabbed at her eyes. "Thank you."

"Don't cry, sweetheart."

"I can't believe you're here taking care of me."

"Did you think I wouldn't?"

"I knew that you would, but I couldn't ask after telling you we have to slow things down and hide our relationship. I don't even know what that means for us."

He used a finger to gently lift her chin to make sure she was looking at him. "Nothing has changed about the way I feel. You can ask me for help. You can count on me, sweetheart."

Her breath shuddered. "It's so nice to have someone take care of me."

"Do you need to go to the doctor? What are your symptoms?"

"No. My doctor already sent out a prescription. Sometimes my seasonal allergies develop into more."

"Is this because we didn't go home for your allergy pill before hiking?"

She ignored that question and ran a hand through her hair. "Ugh. What I must look like."

"Lovely as always."

"I know that's not true. I would love to go take a shower and see if the steam will help my stuffy nose and headache."

"I'll feed everyone breakfast while you do that."

She swung her feet over the side of the bed. "Let me know if you need me."

He needed her, but not in the way she meant. He left her bedroom and peeked into Hallie's room. She was sitting up in her bed.

"Good morning, Hallie." She rubbed her eyes and then silently lifted her arms to him, so he picked her up and settled her against his chest.

"Mommy?"

"Your mommy is taking a shower. Let's go find your sisters." He carried her into the family room. "Lila, can you help Hallie in the bathroom?"

"Sure." She got off the couch and came over to them. "How's Mommy?"

"She's okay. She's taking a shower, and then we can see about getting her to eat something."

"Okay. Come on, Hallie. Let's go potty." She took the toddler's hand shund led her away.

After oatmeal and toast, he got everyone dressed and

checked on JenniLynn. She was sitting on the side of her bed in yoga pants and a pink T-shirt brushing her wet hair. "Are you hungry, sweetheart?"

"Not really."

"How about toast and hot tea and then a nice long sleep while I take care of the kids?"

Her shoulders relaxed and she smiled. "That actually sounds wonderful. I'll come say good morning to the kids and eat and then come back to bed."

Grayson held out a hand and helped her to her feet. He wanted to hold her close, but he resisted and let go of her instead. Not because he was afraid she would get him sick, but because he was afraid of pushing her too far too fast emotionally. He followed her into the family room.

"Mommy!" All three of her girls rushed over to hug her and get reassurance that she was okay. Hallie clung to her for a few extra minutes until she decided she wanted to sit with her dog.

Once JenniLynn was fed and back in bed, he gathered up four children and four dogs, and they all went for a long walk around their ranch. They worked on leash training the puppies, and the mama dog was a surprising help controlling her crew. Sandy walked right beside Hallie, and the other three kids each held a puppy's leash. When they turned around to head home, Hallie got tired and sat down on the ground.

"Adam, will you wear my hat while I carry Hallie on my shoulders?"

"Sure." The black Stetson swallowed the boy's head, but he tipped it back enough to be able to see. "Can I get my own hat soon? My old one is too little."

"That's a good idea. We'll go shopping for one soon." He squatted beside the toddler and lifted her onto his shoulders, but when he stood, she wrapped her arms around his face and whimpered. He gently uncovered his eyes, held both her tiny hands and turned his head to look up at her. "It's okay, Hallie. You don't have to be afraid. I promise I won't let you fall. Are you okay now?"

The two-year-old nodded and visibly relaxed but kept hold of his thumbs and locked her feet across his chest.

"She's never been up that high," Lila said and moved closer to walk beside them.

"Your dad doesn't carry you on his shoulders?"

She shook her head. "No. Not that I can remember."

Grayson bit the inside of his cheek to resist saying something much harsher than their mother's funny curses. What kind of man had three adorable children and had never carried them on his shoulders? He would kill for the kind of family life Rob Garrett gave up. The other man was a complete fool.

On the way back to the house they stopped to gather the eggs and feed the chickens. While the children worked on a puzzle together, he checked on his pretty mayor and found her peacefully sleeping with an eye mask and headphones. Quietly closing her bedroom door, he left her to rest. It made him smile to know she trusted him enough to dull her senses with confidence that he'd look after her girls.

Around lunchtime, he loaded the kids into JenniLynn's SUV and went into town for burgers and ice cream at The Silver Spur Café. It went fairly smoothly, other than the basket of spilled fries when there was a small tussle over where it should sit on the table, and the ice cream that found its way into Hallie's curls.

The waitress brought over the check and a damp cloth for Hallie's hair. "Where is Mayor Garrett today?"

"Mommy is sick in bed," Sasha said. "Mr. Grayson is

taking care of us. Can you believe he knows how to do it without help?"

The waitress held back a laugh. "Wow. That's wonderful."

Grayson handed her his credit card and then cleaned Hallie's hair with the cloth. "Thanks for helping me feed this crew. I'm trying to keep them busy so Mayor Garrett can rest."

An elderly man at a nearby table stood and pushed in his chair. "I think everyone should be thanking you for helping out our mayor when she's in need. She's been through a lot lately. We appreciate you, young man."

He hadn't been called a young man in ages, but this gentleman was probably in his nineties, so he'd take it. "I'm glad I can help her out," Grayson said, as he lifted Hallie from her booster seat.

"It's nice to see a man who can handle so many young kids. Well done," said a lady at another table.

"Thank you, ma'am." This public lunch with the kids was definitely going to make the rumor mill, and he was second guessing his decision to come to town.

He knew JenniLynn was okay with him driving the girls places because he'd done it before, but that was before she'd decided they needed to slow things down between them. His lunch was suddenly not sitting well.

I hope I didn't just sabotage my relationship with Jenni-Lynn even further by parading her girls around town.

It was too late to change things now, and since they'd already made a splash at the café, he decided they might as well go to the grocery store, too. He quickly realized he should have saved the ice cream for *after* the shopping. Hallie was in the shopping cart, but sugared-up energy was making all four kids as bouncy as bunny rabbits.

"Sasha, stop right there. You have to stay in the same aisle with me so I can see you."

"Okay." She spun around before returning to his side and holding onto the cart, but continued to bounce on her toes, making the cart jerk and upsetting her baby sister. Luckily, Sasha stopped before he had to intervene, but in the next aisle, she ran over to a woman he didn't know.

"My mommy is sick, and Mr. Grayson is taking care of us."

The older woman with a white ponytail paused reading the label on a box and smiled at him. "Is that right? How nice of him."

"Just helping out a friend," he said with what he hoped was a smile that didn't look too strained. Or guilty.

"I hope your mommy feels better soon. Tell her I said to call me if she needs anything," she said to Sasha then turned back to him. "Thanks for helping JenniLynn out like this. You're good with the children."

"Thanks. I try."

Lila put a bag of pasta into the cart and held up the shopping list they'd taken off the refrigerator. "That's the last thing on the list."

"Okay, my rowdy bunch. Let's head to the checkout and get home to check on your mommy."

"What's rowdy?" Sasha asked.

"It's when you have lots of energy and are a bit wild."

"Oh. I have lots of energy."

He chuckled, entertained by the way she proudly declared her rowdiness.

On the drive home, he was getting more nervous about telling JenniLynn about their trip to town, but everyone had been thanking him and telling him how good he was with the kids.

"Who was the woman in the store who said to tell your mommy to call her?" he asked the girls.

"That was May Bell Carter," Lila said. "She owns Nothin' New where Mommy shops sometimes. She's really nice and talks to everyone."

Great.

He was going to have the whole town talking. When he confessed to their outing, maybe he should start by telling her about the thanks and compliments he'd received.

Chapter Sixteen

JenniLynn woke to the sound of children's laughter and Grayson trying to shush them, and it made her smile. A few puppies joined in on the action. She stretched and was happy that her head wasn't pounding. She freshened up and then tiptoed out of her bedroom to try to get a look at the Rowdy Bunch in the kitchen before they saw her.

They were making cookies—and a huge mess. The amount of flour dusted around the room was going to require a vacuum, and something sticky dripped from the edge of the counter, but the happiness and joy she saw made her smile. It was the sweetest thing ever.

"Everyone stand back while I open the oven and put them in to bake," Grayson said.

"Mommy! Are you all better?" Sasha asked when she caught sight of her.

"I'm getting there." She smiled at Grayson and mouthed a thank you.

Hallie ran to her. "Mommy."

"Hi, sweet girl." She picked her up and settled her on her hip. "Have you been having a fun day?"

Her toddler nodded and cut a smile Grayson's way. Hallie was slow to warm up to people, but her shy child sure had warmed up to him.

With her chin resting on the countertop, Sasha grinned. "I listened and didn't get in trouble."

"That's good to hear."

"Everyone was very well-behaved," Grayson said.

"Show your mom what we got for her," Adam said.

Lila opened the refrigerator and then put the container on the counter. "We brought you chicken soup from the café."

"Yum. That sounds perfect." The to-go container made her realize what this meant, and a flash of tension swirled in her stomach. "You went to town?"

"We got lunch and groceries, and I should've asked you," Grayson rushed to say. "But you were asleep, and I didn't want to wake you. I'm sorry."

She hated the anxiety making his brow crease. He'd done nothing but help her and she didn't want him to feel bad. "You don't have to be sorry. How did it go?" She hoped he knew what she was really asking. Were there any gossipy incidents?

Sasha hugged her leg. "I told *everyone* Mr. Grayson is taking care of us, and they said he's doing a good job."

JenniLynn saw Grayson wince. "Why don't you kids go play while the cookies bake."

She put Hallie on her feet, and all four kids went into the family room, and Lila turned on the television.

Her handsome cowboy paced in front of the oven, his fingers worrying the denim hems of his blue jeans. Her fear of moving too fast and what people might say had done this to him. One of the last things she wanted to do was cause him stress.

Grayson being here for her when she needed him had made a few things clear. He was the kind of man worth fighting for. He helped her with the girls, but Grayson didn't try to interfere in her decisions or tell her she was parenting wrong—like Rob sometimes had.

She didn't want to rush to negative conclusions that their trip to town was a bad thing, but he was starting to make her nervous. JenniLynn went around to his side of the island and took hold of his hand to make him stop and look at her. "Did something happen you're not telling me?"

"No. The worst that happened was Hallie getting ice cream in her hair. But we did draw a lot of notice."

"The girls seemed to think it was all positive. Tell me about your day out with the Rowdy Bunch." In front of the oven, they both leaned back against the counter, close enough that their arms were touching. She could see their reflection in the glass oven door, and she liked seeing the two of them together like this. At home and casually waiting for freshly baked cookies.

"At the café, an elderly gentleman thanked me for helping you out and another lady said I was good with the children. Then at the grocery store, May Bell Carter said you should call her if you need anything."

"That all sounds good. No questions about the two of us or any snide comments of any kind?"

"Not a one."

"I guess they save all that for me."

He turned to face her. "Has it really been that bad for you, sweetheart?"

She gave it a moment of thought. "Well, I might have overreacted to some of it when I had a killer headache at work. After being linked to my ex's public scandal, I might also be overly sensitive about people talking about my personal life."

"That's completely understandable. We can—"

She put a finger over his lips. "I think the cat is out of the bag, so to speak. There is no way we can pretend we aren't hanging out. I think the Jobs Corps excuse is worn out."

"I told one of the people at the café that I was helping out a friend. I'm sure we can spin it that way."

"Telling them we're friends is the truth. Right?"

He looked over her shoulder to see where the kids were, and when the coast was clear, he gave her a soft kiss. "Of course it's the truth. And the rest is none of their business."

At the moment, she was so grateful for him in her life that she was choosing to believe that everything would work out.

But was this the same thing she'd done with Rob? Choosing to believe it was all fine…until it wasn't? She couldn't completely dismiss that fact, and she promised herself that going forward, she would listen to her instincts.

He opened the oven to check on the cookies. "Speaking of the Jobs Corps, my brother Jesse and my nephew Oscar are coming to town for a visit, and they will be here for the kick-off event we're hosting for the business owners."

"That's great. I can't wait to meet them." Trying to ignore the mess in the kitchen, she got out a bowl, poured her soup into it and put it into the microwave. While it heated, she couldn't resist wetting a rag and wiping up the sticky puddle that was dripping onto the floor.

"Don't worry about that," he said. "I'll clean up while you eat. I'm not going to be responsible for a mess like this and then make you clean it, especially while you're sick."

"I appreciate that offer more than you know."

Rob would have left the mess for her, claiming she could do it better, so why should he bother to help. The instincts she'd just promised to listen to wanted to put another checkmark in Grayson Abernathy's positive-attributes column.

* * *

By that evening, she was feeling much better, and the kids and dogs were playing in the backyard while JenniLynn and Grayson stayed inside and watched the children through the window. They were having what they called Puppy Races. Hallie and Sandy stood at one end of the yard and the older three kids each took a puppy to the other end.

"Ready, set, go!" Adam yelled.

Three puppies were released, and they scampered across the grass to their mom as the kids cheered them on.

JenniLynn laughed. "They sure are having fun."

"The whole Rowdy Bunch seems to be enjoying it. This all worked out just right. Between us, we have the perfect number of dogs and Adam has kids to play with while he's here."

It was impossible to miss the flash of pain on his face. He was dreading the day his son left. JenniLynn put her arm around his waist and lifted onto her toes to kiss his cheek, and Grayson held her snug against his side as if needing the connection.

"Don't hesitate to call me if you start feeling bad again," he said. "Even if it is the middle of the night."

"It means a lot to know that you are only a call away."

"When I was rushing to get to you this morning, I sure did wish I had a gate to get across Mr. Smith's property to yours."

"Were you that worried about me?"

"When you get an early morning wake-up call from two little girls who are worried about their mother, it tends to spur you into action and get your heart revving."

She wrapped both arms around his waist and rested her head on his chest, enjoying being in his embrace. "What did the girls say when they called?"

"That you were sweaty and moaning."

"That's certainly paints a lovely picture of me. You were really scared, weren't you?"

He let out a long slow breath and held her a little tighter. "I really was."

Later that night, all three of her girls were tucked into bed, Sparky was in his crate and Sandy was at the foot of Hallie's new toddler bed. It had been delivered in a big box that had become a super cool spaceship once the kids got ahold of it, and Grayson had put the bed together.

Slipping between the soft, clean sheets, JenniLynn sighed and picked up the book she'd just started and opened it to the bookmarked spot. She'd read one paragraph before she heard little feet in the hallway.

"Mommy," Lila said from the door of the bedroom. "Is it someday?"

"Someday? Come here, sweetie." She lifted the covers and welcomed her little girl in beside her. "Tell me what you mean."

"You said someday you might want a boyfriend, and we see Mr. Grayson and Adam lots. He's really nice and doesn't get upset with Sasha and even Hallie likes him now."

JenniLynn was surprised by her eldest's words. "I thought you didn't want a new father figure. Are you saying you like him being a part of our lives?"

Lila cuddled against her and rested her head on her shoulder. "Mr. Grayson is different than I thought he would be. He's… I don't know how to say it."

"Just tell me whatever you're thinking or feeling. Don't hold back."

"Well… He knows how to have fun and play with kids more than Daddy does. He can take care of me and Sasha and Hallie and Adam all at the same time. All by himself. Daddy can't do that. He has to have Grandma help him."

She was sad to know that her daughter knew that fact. She had hoped the girls hadn't noticed Rob's lack of enthusiasm for parenting.

"I agree that Grayson is very nice and lots of fun." She brushed her fingers through Lila's long silky hair. "To answer your original question. I do like him very much, and I think maybe it is 'someday.' Are you okay with that?"

"He helps you not be so tired and stressed. He helps more than dad did."

JenniLynn tipped up her chin. "But what about you and your sisters? Does he make life better for you, or are you only worried about me?"

"He helps us, too. He can calm Hallie down when she's upset. And he helped me learn how to walk Sparky on a leash and how to start teaching him commands."

"That's great."

"I know us girls are okay on our own, but I think it's okay if Mr. Grayson and Adam get to be in our lives, too."

She hugged her sweet daughter close. "I think so, too. Just remember that Grayson and Adam aren't family members. They are friends that we're still getting to know. I'll have to make sure your sisters understand that."

"I understand, Mommy. I'll remind Sasha that Adam is our friend. Not our brother."

"Maybe we should talk to her about it together," Jenni-Lynn suggested.

"Okay." Lila sighed. "I'm going to miss Adam when he has to go back to his mom's house."

"He'll be back for visits." JenniLynn could only imagine how hard it was going to be for Grayson. He was going to need her support when it was time to take his son home. Knowing the pain he was going to experience broke her heart for him.

The next morning, she sat down beside Sasha on their couch. "When you asked Mr. Grayson to braid your hair, were you testing him just to see if he could do it?"

Her four-year-old cocked her head. "Testing?"

"I'm just curious, why did you go to him and not me to fix your hair?"

Sasha ran her fingers over her braids as if trying to remember. "Well…he knows how to be a dad to a boy kid, and I wanted to see if he knows how to be a good dad for a girl."

"And what did you decide? Is he?"

"Yep. I think so. He's not afraid of girl stuff like glitter and dolls."

She smiled at her daughter, remembering Grayson's sparkly hair when Sasha got gold glitter in it. He had laughed it off and said he didn't think the cows would mind. "Do you like him and Adam being around so much, or do you wish we didn't hang out with them all the time?"

"I like them around. We have fun."

"Sasha, I want you to remember that Mr. Grayson is our good friend, but he is not a new daddy."

"Adam is my friend, too."

"That's right, sweetie."

"Can we go play with Moon Sparkle and Star Sparkle?"

"Maybe later." She chuckled as she remembered Adam's face when he realized Sasha had decided his dogs had to have the same last name as their mom.

"I'm gonna go play in my room." Sasha hugged her. "I love you, Mommy."

"I love you, too, sweet girl."

Even though she needed to get ready for work and everyone ready for daycare, she leaned back on the couch and took a moment to enjoy the feeling of being happy. She wasn't sure about the town of Tenacity, but her family was on board with her relationship with Grayson.

What am I waiting on? I'm a grown woman, and I should stop punishing myself for past mistakes. And listen to my instincts.

Chapter Seventeen

The morning was overcast with a good chance of rain that would be welcomed by every rancher in the area. Grayson had started their day extra early to get a few chores done ahead of any storms that might pop up. They had repaired a section of fence and put out some molasses and mineral blocks for the cattle. He and Adam were now out in the pasture where the herd was grazing. There was a new calf, and both mom and baby were doing well.

"She's so cute," Adam said. "She still has wobbly legs."

"She was just born a few hours ago. They're fun to watch at this age."

A horse neighed, and he turned to see Mr. Smith on horseback riding along the strip of land between his and JenniLynn's ranch. Now was a perfect chance to talk to him. "Adam, sit in the truck while I go talk to the neighbor."

"Okay, Dad."

He waved to Mr. Smith and walked toward the fence line between their ranches. "Good morning."

"Good to see you again, Mr. Abernathy." He dismounted and patted his horse's flank. "How is JenniLynn feeling? I heard you were taking care of the girls for her."

"She's feeling much better. That brings up something I've been wanting to talk to you about. When the girls called before sunrise, told me she was sick and scared the pants off of me, I wished I could drive through here to get to her faster." He motioned from the fence between them to the gate onto her ranch. "Any possibility you would allow me access through your land to drive onto hers? It would save so much time rather than driving around on the road. And I would pay all the expenses to add a gate."

The old cowboy rubbed his fingers over his gray handlebar mustache. "I'll do you one better. Are you interested in buying this twenty-five acre strip between your ranch and hers?"

Grayson felt a bump of excitement. "Yes, sir. I'm very interested."

"I was originally going to sell my whole ranch, but the kids want me to keep the front section with the house and barns. Some of my grandkids want to move to town."

"That's wonderful." He really hadn't wanted to buy an entire ranch with another house to take care of, but adding twenty-five acres of grazing land was a great opportunity. "I would very much like to purchase this section of land." They spent a few minutes talking about price per acre and came to an agreement they were both happy with.

Mr. Smith held his hand across the barbed-wire fence, and they shook. "Pleasure doing business with you, neighbor."

"It certainly is."

"There's no need to wait for the gate. Go ahead and put it in whenever you're ready."

"Thank you so much, Mr. Smith."

The older man started to go but stopped and turned back to Grayson. "I have a question for you. I've been Jenni-Lynn's ranch manager since her divorce, but even though I can still ride a horse, it's time for me to slow down. Would you consider doing it for her?"

"I absolutely would," he answered without a second thought.

"She can't pay much, but it's enough."

"I won't take her money. I have a different trade in mind."

The other man's eyes narrowed. "Maybe you better tell me what that is."

Grayson liked that this man was looking out for her. "Nothing personal," he was quick to say. "Ranch management in exchange for her bull visiting my herd. I've been looking into buying a new one, but this would solve both of our issues."

Mr. Smith chuckled. "I would imagine she will find that deal agreeable, but you'll have to take it up with the lady of Coyote Creek."

"I'll do that." Grayson hooked his thumbs in his front pockets. "I know you've known JenniLynn most of her life and it's obvious you care about her, so I want to be honest with you. I'm crazy about her, and we have been spending a lot of time together."

"I had a feeling. I've seen her face light up when she talks about you." That brought a grin to Grayson's face, and Mr. Smith chuckled. "Kind of like the look on yours right now."

"She does have a way of making my days brighter, but because of what she has been through, we've also been trying to keep it private."

"And you are discovering that's hard to do in a small town?"

"Yes, sir. It sure is."

"There are always going to be folks who talk. It's the way of this old world. Just try to focus on the positive and tune out the rest."

"That's great advice. Thanks."

The old cowboy got back on his horse and rode away. Grayson headed back to the truck where Adam was kicked back with one boot sticking out the open window.

"Sorry, that took longer than I thought," Grayson said as he climbed into the driver's seat and started the truck.

"It's okay. I was playing this old game of yours." He held up the handheld electronic football game that surprisingly still worked.

"Guess what? We just added twenty-five acres to Ambling Hills Ranch."

"We did? How?"

"We are buying that strip of land between our ranch and JenniLynn's."

"That's awesome!" His son shifted in his seat to fully face him. "Now, when the puppies are bigger, they can run back and forth from our house to theirs. Like one big ranch."

One big ranch.

A realization hit him with the force of a tackle. What he wanted was one big, blended family.

Grayson's mind started to swirl with what that might look like. No more setting a timer on the television so it wouldn't be silent when he walked into an empty house at the end of a long day. Having Adam with him had been amazing, and he dreaded the day he went back to his mom's so much that he'd been ignoring the calendar.

Wanting JenniLynn and the girls in his life was much more than just not wanting to be alone, but he wasn't talking about another rush to the altar like he'd done with Rebecca. He did not intend to repeat that mistake, but that didn't mean he wasn't looking forward to someday coming home to people he loved.

He'd fallen completely in love with JenniLynn, and he

adored her sweet girls. He just had to be patient and not push her or the kids or himself, or he risked losing it all.

"When are Uncle Jesse and Oscar getting here?" Adam asked as they parked beside the house.

"They'll be here on Friday night."

"I'm going to clean my room before they get here."

"Great idea."

Adam jumped out and ran toward the house, as if it had to be done at this very moment, and Grayson wasn't going to argue. Before he got to his front door, his phone chimed in his pocket, and the sound he'd programed for JenniLynn made him smile. He stopped in the front yard and pulled it out to read her message.

I'm ready.

A rush of energy washed over him in a wave. Did she mean what he hoped? Was she ready to be not only his friend but his lover? A soft rain started to fall, but he stayed right where he was and sent a quick reply.

Am I supposed to be picking you up for something I've forgotten or are you saying what I hope you are?

Next level ready.

Her reply included a heart emoji and made his own heart beat a little faster. Before he could respond, a second text came through from JenniLynn.

Can you come over tonight for a puppy playdate dinner and we can make plans?

Grayson grinned as he typed, shielding his phone from the rain beneath the brim of his Stetson.

We'll be there, sweetheart.

"Dad," Adam called from the open doorway. "Why are you standing out in the rain?"

He laughed at himself and jogged toward the house.

Because I'm a man in love.

That evening, the Rowdy Bunch played in her front yard under the big tree, and the two of them sat on her porch swing. Grayson was bursting with all the things he wanted to say and ask about their relationship, but he reminded himself that he needed to let her set the pace.

JenniLynn pushed her feet against the porch, making them slowly swing. "Finally, we have a moment alone to talk."

"Don't keep me in suspense, sweetheart. Tell me about our move to the next level."

"Well, I'll tell you how it started. Lila came to me late last night and had lots of good things to say about you. She asked me if you are my boyfriend."

"What did you say?"

"I told her that you are, and she was happy about it."

He took her hand in his and laced their fingers. "That makes me very happy as well. You know Adam is on board with our relationship."

"He is such a dear boy. This morning while I was talking to Sasha, she said she is happy to have you in our lives."

"I'm glad we're all in agreement. I think the dogs will also agree."

She rested her head on his shoulder. "I realized I'm the only one holding us back."

He put his arm around her shoulders. "As I've said from the beginning, you get to set the pace."

She tipped up her face and kissed him softly. "Thanks for being so awesome, cowboy."

"I had an important meeting in my back pasture this morning, and I have some news to share. I also have an offer for you."

"Do tell. I can't wait to hear about an important meeting in the pasture."

"Mr. Smith offered to sell me the twenty-five acre strip of land between our ranches, and we came to a quick agreement. He even told me to go ahead and add a gate." When her eyes widened, he quickly continued. "But I'm not suggesting our ranches become one big ranch or anything like that."

She smiled and kissed him. "It will make it easier to drive back and forth for puppy play dates."

"That was Adam's first reaction, too."

"What is the offer part that involves me?"

"Me becoming your ranch manager so Mr. Smith can retire."

She cocked her head and studied him for a moment. "Do you have time to tend my ranch as well as yours?"

"I do." He might have to hire a few part-time cowboys, but he wouldn't mention that right now. "It's conveniently close."

"That's certainly true."

"Rather than being paid, I would like to borrow your fine bull to add some new blood to my herd."

"I knew your jealousy over my bull would get to you," she teased with a chuckle. "If you're sure it won't be too much for you, I am agreeable to your terms, but I insist on paying you something. And of course I will also help out like I always have."

"You have a deal, Mayor Jenni." He stuck out his hand, but rather than shaking hers, he brought it to his lips and kissed the back of her hand.

"Now that we have all that business taken care of, I think we should discuss something a bit more personal," she said.

"Something else we agree on. Since my brother and nephew will be here on Saturday night, I'll have a babysitter. If you can get one, what do you think about going away for a night after the Jobs Corps kickoff event is over?"

"I think that can be arranged. I'll make a few calls and see who can help me out."

"What about their father?"

She chewed on her thumbnail. "I don't feel comfortable involving him in this. I don't want to see him and then go off with you. I don't want him tainting our time away. Anyway, he would just have his mom take care of them. And she would likely have questions about what I'm doing."

"I can understand that. If this Saturday night doesn't work out, we can pick another. We don't have to rush."

"Maybe I want to rush," she whispered near his ear, making him shiver.

Grayson was about to ask her to step inside so he could give her a proper kiss when one of the girls squealed, and they both looked their way.

"Mommy," Sasha said as she limped toward the porch. "Star tinkled on my foot."

She looked so adorably disgruntled as she perched her fists on her hips that he had to cover his laugh.

JenniLynn got off the swing with her own chuckle. "Come over to the water hose, and we'll wash off your foot."

"I guess it's a good thing she took off her shoes," Grayson said.

"Small blessings," JenniLynn said with a laugh.

Chapter Eighteen

After the boys went home and the girls were in bed, Jenni-Lynn had called everyone, but on such short notice, she couldn't find anyone to stay with the girls who Hallie would be comfortable with. With her stomach in knots, she made the call she didn't want to make.

"Hello."

The sound of her ex-husband's voice made her stomach clench into knots, and she paced around the kitchen island. "Hi, Rob."

"Are the girls okay?"

"Yes. They're all doing great. Can you come stay with them on Saturday night?"

"Where are you going?" His voice held the accusatory tone she hated.

"I need to go to Bronco," she said, trying to keep her own voice calm and natural.

"For what?"

Her anger was rising. Why couldn't the man just be excited about an opportunity to spend time with his own children? He was quiet for a moment, hopefully realizing he'd lost his right to ask her what she was doing or where she spent her time. "Does it matter?"

"I guess not."

Sandy came into the room and gave a soft bark that meant she needed to be let outside, and JenniLynn opened the back door.

"Did I just hear a dog?" Rob asked.

"You did. We adopted a mama dog and her puppy."

"The dog is in the house? Our old dog was a ranch dog who stayed outside."

"Things change." She wanted to yell at him that it was none of his damn business, and that this was no longer his house. He had shot that right straight to hell, but instead, she bit her tongue because she didn't feel like fighting with him. "Sandy is a well-trained therapy dog, and she is great in the house."

"Why a therapy dog?"

"Because she and Hallie bonded."

"Is something wrong with Hallie that you aren't telling me?"

"Why would you even ask that?"

"Because she doesn't talk like she used to. She isn't the same as our older two girls."

Her temper spiked. When anyone said something negative about one of her babies, the mama bear came out in her. It was all up to her to do what was best for her girls, and Rob didn't know *shit* about anything.

"JenniLynn? Are you still there?"

She took a deep breath. "Every child is different. She's shyer than Lila and Sasha and has them to talk for her. There is absolutely nothing wrong with Hallie that you didn't have a hand in with all the upheaval and stress over this past difficult year." That seemed to shut him up. "Can you come take care of your children or not?"

"Yes, I can. Mom and I will come and stay the night on Saturday."

She wasn't surprised that he was bringing backup, but the girls would love seeing their grandmother. "Thank you. I have a town event the girls want to attend in the middle of the day, but if you could come to the house in the late afternoon or early evening that would be perfect."

"I'll see you Saturday."

"Goodbye," she said in a professional manner like she would do from her office and then hung up. She growled at the phone like she'd wanted to do to him.

It took her several minutes, a glass of wine and cuddling with the puppy to calm down after her conversation with Rob. But she knew what would really make her feel better. She called Grayson.

"Hi, sweetheart."

His deep voice instantly soothed her frazzled nerves. "Hi. I couldn't wait to tell you my news. I was able to get babysitting for Saturday night."

"That's great. Who did you find to take care of the girls?"

She ground her back teeth together. "Rob and his mom are coming to stay with them."

"Grandma is coming?" Sasha asked excitedly from behind her.

JenniLynn spun to face her. "Yes, she is, but why are you out of bed, young lady?"

"Uhm… I'm just checking on you, Mommy. Goodnight." She ran back to her bedroom.

"Did you hear that?" she asked Grayson.

"I did. And I noticed she didn't say anything about her dad coming."

"Sad, isn't it?"

"JenniLynn, I'm really glad you got babysitting, but are you sure you're okay with this? We can plan something for a later date."

"I'm okay. It's something I need to get used to, and this might as well be the first step."

"I'm proud of you, Mayor Jenni."

That made her smile. "Thanks. I needed to hear that. Everything is ready for the Jobs Corps kickoff event. I even wrote a speech to give to all the business leaders, but I need to work on it some more."

"I can't wait to hear it. Adam and I will be in town around noon tomorrow. Can we bring you lunch at your office? I can help you and Monica go over the final details for the event."

The whole town was already talking about them, and all four children were happy with the current arrangement. What was the point of continuing to hide their relationship? She'd gotten through everything with Rob and the election scandal, and if there was a stir about her personal life, she'd get through that, too. It would be nothing more than a blip on the radar after what she'd dealt with.

She was tired of hiding.

"That would be nice," she told him. "Now I better go put my daughter back to bed."

"Tell her I said to have sweet dreams."

"I will."

"Sweet dreams to you, too."

"Good night, honey." She'd never called him that before, but it felt right. She hung up with a smile on her face and love in her heart.

Sitting on her bed after assuring herself Sasha was asleep, she thought about her phone calls with Rob and Grayson. The contrast was obvious. The conversation with her ex had been tense with an accusatory tone and made her stress level rise. With Grayson, it was all calm and supportive, making her want to draw this handsome cowboy all the way into their lives.

Could she trust her instincts to lead her in the right direction? Was she ready to tell Grayson that he was stealing her heart, or should she continue to guard it?

JenniLynn had called him honey, and it made a special kind of warmth spread through his entire body. "I should get flowers for her."

"Dad, who are you talking to?" Adam's hair was wet from his shower, and he looked so cute in his striped pajamas.

He chuckled. "Just myself. Are you sure you're okay with me going away with JenniLynn while Jesse and Oscar are here?"

"Yep. I'm sure. She's a super cool lady."

"I'm glad you think so, and I agree."

Adam tapped his bare foot on the floor as if coming to a decision about something. "I think she needs you."

"Why do you say that?"

"Because she has lots of people and stuff to take care of for one person. And she really likes you. She smiles at you with lovey eyes and stuff." He tried to imitate JenniLynn by smiling and fluttering his eyelashes and made Grayson grin. "You smile at her, too, Dad."

"Oh, yeah? What do I look like when I smile at her?"

Adam held back his shoulders, cocked his head and gave a squinty eyed smile that ended with a little nod.

He laughed. "You notice everything, don't you? You're one smart kid."

"My teacher last year said I'm smart."

"Let's get you tucked into bed so your brain can grow even bigger while you sleep." He tossed Adam over his shoulder and made his little boy laugh as he carried him to bed.

As soon as he was alone, Grayson started officially making the plans he'd been making in his head. He booked a room at one of the nicest hotels in Bronco and then made a reservation for dinner at a fancy restaurant. He was planning on pulling out all the stops for their first night together, and if it felt right, he would tell her he'd fallen in love.

In The Silver Spur Café around noon on Friday, Grayson and Adam were talking about the newest baby calf while they waited for their to-go lunch order.

The elderly gentleman who'd thanked him for helping JenniLynn the day she was sick stopped in front of them. "Where are those cute little girls?"

"They're at daycare today."

He patted Grayson's shoulder with surprising strength. "Good to see you again."

"You, too, sir."

A middle-aged waitress with curly blonde hair in a pony-tail handed him their order in a large paper bag with handles. "I added a few cookies free of charge. They are Mayor Garrett's favorite."

"Thank you. How did you know some of this food is for her?"

"Because that's the way she likes her salad and…" She shrugged. "You two seem to be…close."

He chuckled. "Maybe you should be a detective."

"I tell my husband that all the time," she said with a cheery laugh. "There's a cookie in there for you, too, young man." She winked at Adam.

"Thanks," his son said before the woman hurried back into the kitchen. "I like this town. At the restaurants near Mom's house, they don't give free cookies. I love cookies."

"I like it here, too." The sweet thing that Grayson craved

was not the treat in the bag. It was the woman who had scored them the free cookies. And he couldn't wait to see her.

As they walked up to Tenacity Town Hall, Adam pointed to the clock tower on the old brick building. "That's not the right time."

"JenniLynn said the clock hasn't worked in years. Maybe I should see what it would take to get it fixed."

A man in a suit rushed out the front door on his phone and almost ran into them. Grayson sidestepped, and the other man stopped.

"Sorry about that, Mr. Abernathy."

"No problem." It was Billy Riley, the city council member who asked JenniLynn out. He looked like he wanted to say more, so Grayson waited.

"I think I know a business owner who might want to work with you and the Jobs Corps."

"That's great. Send me their information."

"I will. Say hi to JenniLynn for me," he said and went on his way.

Grayson was glad to see that the townsfolks seem to be getting on board with his and JenniLynn's relationship.

"Can I knock on the big door?" Adam said as they neared her office.

"Sure."

Grayson silently chuckled as his nine-year-old straightened his shirt, as if knocking on the mayor's door was important business.

"Come in," JenniLynn called out to them.

"Hello, Mayor Garrett," his son said as they entered.

"Hi, Adam. I'm so glad you could come visit me at work today."

Grayson put the food on the table. "Are you glad to see me, too?"

"I am."

"Some lady at the restaurant sent you free cookies," Adam said as he looked out the windows onto Central Avenue.

"Oh, good. I've been craving something sweet," she said while looking directly at Grayson with a sexy smile.

He loved it when they thought alike.

Monica came out of her small office and joined them at the conference table, where the four of them ate and discussed the last few details for the Jobs Corps kickoff event. Before they left, Grayson was able to sneak in one kiss while Adam was in the bathroom and Monica was back in her office. It would have to do until he could get some alone time with her.

Later that afternoon, Grayson was preparing one of the recipes JenniLynn had taught him to make while they waited for Jesse and Oscar to arrive. His brother would be surprised that he'd cooked, but he would likely be just as surprised when he told him about JenniLynn.

"Dad, they're here," Adam yelled.

He put the macaroni and cheese into the oven to bake and went outside with Adam and waved as they parked. As soon as they were out of the truck, he pulled his younger brother into a big bear hug. "I'm so glad you two are here."

"It's good to finally be here, big brother. Your ranch is beautiful. I can't wait for a tour of the whole place."

"Thanks. I love it here." When it came to Oscar, he knew to hug him just lightly enough to let him know he cared without overwhelming him with too much physical contact. "It's so good to see you."

"You, too, Uncle Grayson. I'm looking forward to checking out the job program you put together."

"I'm glad you're here to be a part of it. You are my inspiration, kiddo."

"Oscar, want to see my new room?" Adam said.

"Sure. Help me unload our stuff first."

They all grabbed something and made it inside in one trip, and he got them each settled in a guest room. For once, all four of his bedrooms would be filled.

"Jesse, let's grab a cold drink and catch up," Grayson said.

In the backyard, the boys played with the puppies while they sat in the shade. The sun was going down and filling the sky with warm colors, and a cool evening breeze made it comfortable.

Jesse twisted the cap off his bottle. "There's something I want to talk to you about."

"You sound serious. Is something wrong?"

"No. Not unless you don't want me around more often."

"I always want you around. What's up?"

"I'm thinking about moving here to Tenacity."

"That's wonderful news." Grayson clasped his brother's shoulder and gave it a squeeze. Jesse had been a widower for about ten years now, and a new start was probably just what he needed. "Having you and Oscar close would be great. He can be part of the Jobs Corps. And since he's showing an interest in football, I can work with him."

"He would like that."

"And of course you guys can stay with me until you can get settled. My house is open to you whenever you're ready."

"Thanks. That will make things much easier."

Grayson leaned back in his chair, took a sip of his drink and looked around at his new home. "This house is obviously big enough for a whole family, and after growing up in a family the size of ours, I'm tired of being alone."

"I was wondering when you'd get to this point."

"Dad, we're hungry," Adam said as he ran up to them wiping the sweat from his forehead. "Can we grill the steaks now?"

"Sure. I'll get the grill heated up."

One beer later, the savory scent of steaks filled the kitchen as Jesse carried them inside and put them on the table. Grayson used his knee to close the oven door and put the pan on a hot pad beside the meat.

Jesse eyed the baked macaroni and cheese. "Who made that?"

"I did," Grayson said with a grin.

His brother and nephew shared a look of fear. "But you can't cook," they both said.

"His girlfriend taught him how to make it, and it's actually good," Adam announced.

"Girlfriend? Why don't I know about this?" Jesse asked and took his seat.

"Because it's new." Grayson put a steak and a scoop of mac and cheese on Adam's plate.

"Well, it's about time," Jesse said.

"The secret is out now. And if Dad marries JenniLynn, I'll have three sisters," Adam said, with a grin that was kind of like looking into a mirror.

Grayson ruffled his son's hair. "Whoa. You need to slow down with the marriage talk. And I thought you said you could keep a secret?"

"Come on, Dad. I knew you'd tell Uncle Jesse. Isn't that what brothers do?"

There was a pinching sensation in his heart. His son wanted siblings, and he wanted them for him. "Yes, it is. But not just brothers. You can tell sisters things, too."

"That's true," Jesse said and cut into his steak. "I talk to

Amanda and Evie when I need advice from a girl's point of view. But let's get back to this new girlfriend. This is something I need to hear more about. Start at the beginning."

He and Adam filled them in on getting to know the Garrett girls and had them laughing with their tales about Sasha. After dinner, the boys helped clean up and started playing a video game in the living room while Grayson and his brother took the puppies outside to run around for a few minutes before bed.

The sky was clear, and billions of stars shimmered above them. The night was alive with the sounds of nature and nocturnal animals moving about. A family of raccoons chattered in a nearby tree, and an owl swooped across the backyard.

Grayson stroked the soft fur of the sleeping puppy in his lap. "I know you two just got here, but would you mind looking after Adam tomorrow night so I can go away with JenniLynn for the night?"

"I'm happy to do it, brother. You know that. I really am happy to see you so excited about a woman. We've all been waiting for you to put yourself back out there."

"I was just waiting for the right one. JenniLynn is sweet and fierce and beautiful inside and out. Instead of cussing, she says things like fudgesicle and spadoodle."

"She sounds amazing." Jesse clinked his beer bottle against Grayson's. "I can't wait to meet her."

"You'll love her."

"Do you? Love her I mean."

Grayson's skin tingled from head to toe. "Yes. Heaven help me, but I do."

"Does she?"

"I don't know yet, but it's my ultimate hope. She's recently divorced, so we're trying to go slow. I don't want to push her too fast."

"Good plan. Don't push yourself too fast either. I understand why you jumped so quickly into things with Rebecca. I just want you to make the right choice for the right reasons this time."

"It's not like that with JenniLynn. There is no hurry to make anything official."

"That's good to hear. Other than a woman and three little girls in your life, what else is new?"

"I'm buying twenty-five more acres of grazing land, and once I own it, my ranch will share a fence line with Jenni-Lynn's ranch."

"If you two don't stay together, that could be awkward."

"I'll just have to make sure that doesn't happen."

He sent up a wish to the brightest star above them that their love was written among them.

Chapter Nineteen

By midmorning on Saturday, the auditorium of Tenacity Town Hall was set up for the Jobs Corps kickoff event. The tables were decorated with white tablecloths and fresh flowers. A local man was softly playing an acoustic guitar in the corner where he would later sing while they ate lunch, and a variety of Jobs Corps swag was spread out on a table in the back near the buffet line. Her girls looked so pretty in their matching pink dresses. They were reading books together at one of the tables at the front of the room nearest to the podium where she'd speak.

As the crowd formed, she could see Monica's stress level rising, even though the young woman was doing a good job of trying to hide it. "Monica, there is a stack of important paperwork on the center of my desk. Would you like to go work on it until it's time for the event to start?"

"Sure, Mayor Garrett. Text me if you need me to come back to the auditorium sooner."

"I will." She had saved the stack of paperwork for just this possibility and was glad to give Monica a few minutes of quiet.

JenniLynn's own stress level was higher than normal, and she wasn't sure why. Maybe it was the speech she had to give or that she'd have to see her ex face-to-face in a few hours. Maybe it was nerves about going away with Grayson. She hadn't been with anyone other than Rob.

"Mommy, they're here," Sasha shouted.

She held her finger to her lips to remind her daughter not to shout, and then she turned to see Grayson and Adam with another man and a teenager who looked enough like them to let her know they were family. The smile on Grayson's handsome face made some of her stress start to melt away. She had backup, and knowing that lifted some of the weight from her shoulders.

Introductions were made and her girls were excited to meet new people. At least Lila and Sasha were. Hallie hid behind her and clung to her gray skirt.

"Oscar, I'm so glad you can be here for this. Your uncle is very proud of you and talks about you all the time."

The teenager smiled but didn't hold her gaze. "He's a pretty great uncle."

Hallie and Sasha started squabbling over a toy, and she excused herself to deal with it. "Girls, this is not the place for that kind of behavior. Share or I'm putting the toy away."

"Okay, Mommy. I'll be good while you work," Sasha said, but Hallie crossed her little arms over her chest and stuck out her bottom lip.

Grayson brushed his hand against hers. "Everything looks great. How are you feeling?"

"I've been a little stressed, but I'm better now that you're here."

He leaned in close to whisper, "Everything I have planned for tonight will melt *all* our stress away."

The tingly heat of a blush flushed her skin. "I can't wait."

People began to file into the auditorium, so they went in opposite directions to greet their guests.

When JenniLynn took the stage to give her opening remarks and speech, she looked out at the crowd of smiling faces and her throat tightened, but then her gaze settled on the table right in front of her, and she was able to start without a trembling voice.

"Welcome, everyone. Thank you all for being here today, and for being part of this wonderful program. Let me start by saying, it wouldn't be possible without the ideas of Grayson Abernathy." She swept out her hand toward him where he sat with his family and her girls.

Her tall cowboy stood and waved with an adorably shy smile, and everyone cheered and clapped.

Hallie slapped her hands over her ears and shook her head. Lila patted her back, but it didn't seem to be helping.

Fingers crossed that her toddler would calm down, JenniLynn continued to thank people and went on with her speech, but she couldn't help but see Hallie getting more agitated. Grayson was whispering to her and trying to calm her, but Hallie arched her back and cried out.

It was the worst time possible for her toddler to have one of her meltdowns. She couldn't leave her podium to deal with it, but thankfully Grayson picked her up and carried her out of the room. Grateful for his help, she finished her speech and directed everyone to help themselves to the catered buffet that included food from several local restaurants.

She slipped out into the hallway where Grayson was walking back and forth with Hallie resting on his chest, probably getting tearstains on his sapphire-blue button-up shirt. "Thank you so much for tending to her."

"Of course. I'm sorry I missed your speech."

"It's okay."

Hallie lifted her head and reached for her. "Mommy."

"Hi, sweetie. Are you hungry?" Hallie nodded and cuddled against her.

"Let's go get some food," he suggested, and they went back into the event together. "You sit down with Hallie, and I'll take the girls through the buffet line, and we'll bring you a plate."

"That would be great." She took a seat between Sasha and Lila. "You two go with Adam and get some food, and we'll wait here."

"Okay, Mommy." Sasha leaned in to kiss both her and Hallie's cheek then took Lila's hand and followed the rest of them across the room. Her mischievous child was working so hard to be good for her mommy on an important day.

People seemed to realize she was tending to her child and didn't come bother them. "Are you feeling better now, sweet girl?"

Hallie looked up at her and sighed. "Eat, Mommy."

"Your food will be here in just a couple of minutes." She kissed her blond curls. She was just hungry. That's all it was. But it made her feel like she hadn't been a good mom today. She'd been so busy trying to make sure this event went well that she hadn't given her youngest daughter a snack.

The rest of the event went smoothly, and everyone enjoyed the food and music. She was able to spend some time mingling with people and not one person had said a single thing about her and Grayson sharing the table like a family. No staring and whispering. No one asking if they were dating or any gossipy, nosey comments.

Had everyone accepted them being together, and they could now move on and live life normally?

Once everyone had gone, and there were only a few people cleaning up, JenniLynn boxed up the leftover swag that had been spread out on a table at the back of the room. The girls were sitting with Grayson, Adam and Oscar. Jesse was standing in front of them animatedly telling them a story and making them laugh. It sounded like something about when Grayson was a little boy.

She wanted to join them and laugh along, but she needed a moment alone. She was dreading seeing Rob in just a little while. She reminded herself to be strong and not to let him set her off with some stupid comment. He was not going to mess up her time with Grayson. If she just got through her interaction with him quickly, she and Grayson could be on their way to Bronco.

She glanced over her shoulder at her cowboy and her little girls, and her heart felt so full. She was looking forward to their getaway, and she'd packed her prettiest lingerie. She was so excited about being alone with him. A man who was sweet and thoughtful and funny. He pitched in to help without having to be asked, and he always seemed to know when she needed a little extra encouragement.

And best of all, he never told her what she was doing wrong or pretended he knew more about what the girls needed than she did.

Please let tonight go well. She smiled at Grayson as he crossed the room to her.

He put an arm around her shoulders and gave her a quick squeeze. "You done good, Mayor Jenni. I think everyone is excited about the program."

"I couldn't have done it without you. And you saved the day by helping me with Hallie."

"You know I'm there for all four of you. I think the crowd and the noise was probably just too much for Hallie."

JenniLynn was once again hit with working-mother guilt. Lila and Sasha had been excited about watching Mommy work, but she hadn't really considered that Hallie might not feel that way.

Grayson's question interrupted her thoughts. "What's wrong, sweetheart?"

"Sometimes I just worry that with my work, I'm not giving the girls enough attention."

"You haven't done anything wrong." He opened a door beside him. "Let's go in here for a minute."

"Okay." Curious what was going on, she followed him into a small, empty conference room off the auditorium.

"Would you consider getting Hallie evaluated?" he asked her.

She stared at him, waiting for him to say more. "For what?"

"I think Hallie is dealing with some sensory issues."

"She was just hungry."

"She's also exhibiting some neurodivergent behaviors consistent with autism spectrum."

JenniLynn gasped and recoiled from him. *No! Not another man who thinks he knows my girls better than me.*

"Jenni, look at me, sweetheart." He stepped closer, but she moved away from him. "I didn't mean to upset you or overstep."

"This is crazy. This is *not* my daughter. She's just quiet and shy and maybe a late bloomer."

"You know from the work we've done together that autism is a big spectrum."

"Why would you put my baby on this spectrum?"

"I've noticed certain behaviors."

She wrapped her arms across her waist, as if she could hold herself together. "Like what?"

"Not engaging in conversation or making eye contact. Lining up her toys instead of playing with them. Melting down when things get too noisy or people get too close.

There are other signs. But, sweetheart, there is nothing to worry about. I can suggest some professionals who can help. I'll help you schedule appointments and—"

"You're just seeing diagnoses everywhere and this whole event today has it on your mind. You're searching for signs of something because of your work with the foundation, but not everyone has issues that you need to fix."

He held up both hands and nodded his head. "You're right. It could be that it's on my mind with Oscar visiting and today's event. Let's just forget about this."

JenniLynn straightened her spine. She was not going to have another man in her life who didn't know her girls a fraction of the way she did telling her he knew what was best. If she'd learned anything, it was that she had to be self-sufficient. She could not let him take over.

She could not rely on anyone but herself.

"But you think it," she said. "You think something is wrong with my baby."

"There is nothing *wrong* with Hallie. There is nothing wrong with different ways of learning and thinking and engaging with the world."

She couldn't meet his eyes. "Maybe tonight is a bad idea."

"JenniLynn, please don't say that."

She needed to spend more time with her girls and focus on them and her job. She shouldn't be getting involved with someone right now. "I have too much at stake. I just can't do this right now. It's not good timing for…us."

"Jenni—"

"I'm sorry, Grayson. For now, I need to focus on my family and my job."

He winced and his face turned ashen. Her heart felt as if it was being crushed by a vise, but she had to be strong.

Chapter Twenty

JenniLynn opened the door and left Grayson standing alone in an empty conference room. With his heart breaking into pieces.

What did I just do?

In a numb kind of fog, he forced himself to move forward and followed her to the table where everyone was waiting on them. Grayson didn't want her to throw away what they had because she was scared. Scared of something being wrong with her child. Scared of trusting another man with her heart.

But what could he do? He'd told her over and over that they would go at her pace. Ultimately, this was JenniLynn's decision, and he had to accept it.

Why did I open my big mouth and overstep when it comes to her kids? Especially today of all days.

She had pasted on a bright smile and was gathering up her girls. "We need to get home before your dad and grandma get there."

Her ex-husband. He and his mother were supposed to be staying at her house tonight. Was she going to let him stay there with her or send him home? Would she cry on his shoulder? Grayson's stomach twisted into knots.

There were a few uncomfortable minutes as they gathered up their things.

As they all walked out to the parking lot, Jesse slowed down to walk beside him at the back of the group. "Is everything okay?"

"No," he said under his breath. "I'll tell you later."

Thankfully, none of the kids seemed to pick up on any of the tension.

Knowing Grayson's mind was elsewhere, Jesse got into the driver's seat, and they headed for home. For the whole ride Grayson beat himself up for ruining not just tonight but possibly everything.

"When are you leaving, Dad?"

"Well, buddy. It turns out that JenniLynn needs to stay home with her girls tonight. I get to hang out with you guys instead." He hoped his smile was convincing.

"Is it because Hallie got so upset?" Adam asked.

"Yes." It was the truth, just not in the way his son meant.

As soon as they got inside the house, he went into his bedroom. Flopping back onto his bed, Grayson covered his face and groaned. "This sucks so bad."

There was a knock at his door. "It's Jesse. Let me in."

"It's open."

His brother came inside with a bottle of whiskey and two glasses and sat on the foot of the bed beside him. "Want to tell me, or just drink?"

"Let's start with a drink." He accepted the glass and took a sip. He rarely drank hard liquor, but he welcomed the burn of it going down his throat. "Your big brother is a stupid man who doesn't know how to keep his mouth shut."

"What did you say to her?"

"I stuck my nose in her business where it doesn't belong. I sure could've used some of that sisterly guidance we were telling Adam about. Too bad neither of our sisters was around to give advice about what *not* to say to a mama bear."

Jesse swirled the amber liquid in his glass and then took a sip. "Surely your fight will blow over soon."

"We'll see." At the moment, Grayson was short on hope.

On the way home, JenniLynn had turned up the radio and let the girls sing along to their favorite songs so they wouldn't ask her any questions. With her heart aching so badly, she had needed the time to think and focus on the road.

Now that she was standing in the middle of her family room, what in the hell was she supposed to do? She certainly didn't want to stay here with her ex-husband while she mourned the relationship that had just blown up in her face. She didn't want to admit to anyone that her plans had been canceled. Not even to herself.

Rob's trial was starting soon, reminding her of how he'd betrayed her. The man she was married to! How could she be sure she wasn't making another mistake, putting her faith in a new man after so little time? Maybe she'd totally misread her own feelings, and her relationship with Grayson really was just one of those rebounds people talked about.

She needed to stop standing here moping and make a new plan. First things first, she'd get the girls settled. Then she'd take her suitcase out to the car so she wouldn't have to answer any questions about it. When Rob got here, she would tell him what he needed to know and then drive away.

To where, she had no idea.

The girls were in the front yard waiting with the dogs when their dad and grandmother drove up a little while later. She called upon her very best acting skills and greeted her ex-mother-in-law with a smile and a hug. "Thanks so much for coming."

"I'm thrilled to spend time with the girls."

The best she could do with Rob was a nod and a brief hello. She gave them a few instructions, kissed her girls goodbye and told them she would see them by lunchtime tomorrow. JenniLynn grabbed her purse, went outside and drove away. The fancy dress she'd planned to wear to dinner was still hanging in her closet—where they'd first kissed.

And now, she might never kiss Grayson again.

She drove through town and kept on driving. Still too numb to cry, she let the country radio station play sad songs while she stared straight ahead. An hour or so down the highway, she saw a roadside motel with a vacancy sign flashing and pulled into the parking lot. The room was old but clean enough, and she let her suitcase drop to the floor at the foot of the bed.

This was a far cry from the nice room she would've shared with Grayson. This was everything tonight should *not* have been. She was alone. Her heart was breaking because she'd given it away too soon, and her world was spinning out of control.

It was too quiet, so she turned on the television just to fill the space with something other than her own miserable thoughts. She unzipped her suitcase, but the first thing she saw was the silky pink nightie she'd planned to wear for her first time alone with Grayson.

Instead, she pulled her dress off over her head and crawled into bed in her underwear and covered her head.

Rather than soft sheets and the spicy scent of Grayson's cologne, the room smelled of microwaved food and the sheets were cheap and scratchy. The abrasiveness against her skin that should have been getting caressed by Grayson's hands was the final push that broke the dam, and JenniLynn's tears flowed until she drifted into a fitful sleep.

Rather than waking up beside a beautiful woman he loved, Grayson was rudely awakened by a killer headache and a world-class hangover. Another stupid thing he'd done to himself.

After coffee and pain relievers, he got up the courage to call JenniLynn, but she didn't answer, and he hung up without leaving a message. He just wanted to know that she was okay, but he didn't know what to say other than sorry. And that didn't seem like enough.

Over the next couple of days, he went through the motions. Smiling and laughing when appropriate and finding moments alone to mope about the state of his love life. Jesse and Oscar had kept him busy, but now they were gone. And before he knew it, Adam would be leaving as well.

Grayson's whole body ached from carrying around so much tension. He couldn't let himself fall into a depression, like he'd done after his divorce. He had to keep moving.

He sat on the couch beside his son. "I guess you've noticed we haven't seen JenniLynn and the girls."

"What happened, Dad?" He shifted on the cushion to fully face him.

"Well, we had a disagreement over something. My fault, I'm afraid."

"Are you going to make up with her?"

"I sure hope so. I'm going to try. I think she just needs more time than me to be ready to be boyfriend and girlfriend."

Please let that be true.

"I miss hanging out with the girls and their dogs."

"I know you do, buddy." He tried to swallow the lump in his throat. "I'm sorry I messed everything up."

Adam climbed onto his knees and hugged him. "It's okay. We'll be just fine, Dad."

He held his sweet boy tight against his chest. "Yes, we will. I love you."

"Love you, too."

Grayson missed JenniLynn desperately. He missed her girls, and so did Adam. But right now, he was going to focus on every minute he had left with his son.

Chapter Twenty-One

JenniLynn was miserable, but for the past couple of days, she'd focused all her attention and energy on her girls and work. She kept busy from dawn to dark. Working in the office, at home and outside around her ranch. She had decided she would be her own ranch manager. With Monica's help at work, she could do it. She would add a part-time farm hand to do some of the heavier upkeep. Staying busy would be good for her. Maybe then she would be so exhausted at night that she could fall asleep without thinking about Grayson.

Lila and Sasha kept asking when Adam and Mr. Grayson were coming back, and she kept making excuses. Holding off deeper questions was only going to last for so long, and she needed to decide what to tell them. That, however, required that she knew what she wanted to do. What she *should* do.

It was in the quiet moments when she soaked in the tub or tried to sleep, that she missed Grayson desperately and the tears would fall. He had called several times, but she couldn't bring herself to answer until she figured a few things out.

The same worries kept swirling around and around in her mind. Grayson had taken some of the weight from her shoulders and jumped in to be her backup when needed. Like a stand-in parent. She could call him at a moment's notice, and if at all possible, he would be there for her. And if that wasn't enough, he had been willing to double his workload by managing her ranch, too.

As crazy as it sounded for those things to be worries, they posed an important question she needed to answer.

Had she just fallen for him because he made life easier for her?

Grayson had called JenniLynn several times, but he still hadn't heard from her. Not even a text or a missed call. A couple of times, he had almost left a message, but the things he wanted to say to her couldn't be done through technology.

So, this morning, he'd decided that he would completely back off, giving her all the space she needed to figure things out. The next move was up to her. At least that was what he was telling himself today.

He put down the sandwich he'd only taken one bite of and sighed. His stomach was twisted into too many knots to eat. Leaving his uneaten meal on the kitchen counter, he went into the living room to turn on the television and check the weather.

His phone rang, and he fumbled to grab it quickly in case it was JenniLynn, but he knocked it off the coffee table and onto the floor. When he finally picked it up and looked at the screen, he was disappointed. Again. It was his ex-wife.

He let out a long sigh and then answered. "Hello, Rebecca."

"Hi, Grayson. How's everything going? How's our boy?"

"He's great. We are having lots of fun. Everything okay with you?"

"I have some news I need to talk to you about. Do you have time right now?"

"Sure. What's up?"

"I received a really amazing job offer."

"That's wonderful. Congratulations, Rebecca. Is it the one you wanted?"

"Not exactly. It's an even bigger promotion, but…it's in Europe."

The bottom dropped out of his world, and he sat down hard on the recliner behind him. His next breath lodged painfully in his lungs. "Did you say Europe? As in overseas?"

"Grayson, don't get upset. Listen to my proposal first. This is harder for me than you know."

He took a few deep breaths to calm his pounding heart. "I'm listening."

"Rather than uprooting him in such a big way, how would you feel about Adam living with you and going to school in Tenacity while I'm overseas?"

"Really?" He shot to his feet. "I would love that."

They continued to discuss how it would work while she and her husband were overseas. They came to an agreement he was thrilled with and then he put the phone on speaker, and they included their son in the conversation.

"I'll get to go to the same school as my friend Lila," he told his mom.

"That's so great that you will already know someone."

"I met some guys when I played flag football. So, I'll know them, too."

While Adam continued talking to his mom, Grayson drifted into his own thoughts. His son would be living with him full-time. This was amazing news, and he was so excited and already thinking about registering Adam at the elementary school. He would ask JenniLynn about—

He grimaced and cut that thought off before finishing it.

He might have to navigate all this without her. His house would be a home with his son here, but his arms would still be empty each night if he didn't find a way to fix things with the woman he loved.

The next day at work, JenniLynn was exhausted but pushed through to mid-afternoon, when she'd had all she could take. She went to the door of Monica's office. "Will you be okay if I leave early today?"

"Of course. I'll handle everything."

"You are a superstar." Monica's usually timid smile suddenly looked so proud, and JenniLynn loved seeing this young woman blossoming.

"Go get your girls and make it an early night so you can get some rest. You've been working too hard."

JenniLynn almost hugged her amazing secretary before she remembered that the young woman wasn't a hugger. "I'll do just that. Thanks."

She arrived at Little Cowpokes Daycare Center earlier than usual and said hello to a few people as she signed the girls out. When she went into the toddler room where Hallie was, she took a moment to observe her with her peers before Hallie realized she was there. Her daughter sat alone, happily lining up wooden blocks and paying no mind to anyone else.

In a room full of two-year-olds, Hallie's mannerisms suddenly set her apart from the other toddlers. They were all engaging *with* one another. They were making eye contact and chattering away about their shared toys.

The realization hit JenniLynn like a lightning bolt, and she gasped with the force of it. Everything became crystal clear.

Grayson is right!

Too numb to move, she just stood there watching her baby. It was then that she thought about the young woman she'd left in charge of the mayor's office. She was able to recognize the neurodivergent signs in Monica and had happily made accommodations for her as needed.

Why hadn't she been able to see it in her own child?

Grayson had been right about something else. There was nothing *wrong* with Hallie. She was the same precious child she had always been. No label could ever change that or limit how far her daughter could go in life.

Hallie finally saw her and got up to run to her. Scooping her up, she hugged her close to her chest. "I love you, sweet girl."

"Squishing me, Mommy."

"I'm sorry. You are just so huggable." She settled her on her hip and kissed her rosy cheek.

"JenniLynn, I keep meaning to tell you how good Grayson was with your girls while you were sick," said Elaina Bernard, one of the women who ran the daycare.

She cleared her throat to make sure her voice would work. "He is really good with them."

Angela Corey, the other manager, walked over to join them. "You've got a rare gem in that cowboy. Don't let that man get away, honey."

JenniLynn looked back and forth between the two women, trying to read their expressions. They seemed completely sincere. "You don't think it's too soon?"

"No," they both said in unison.

"You've been through the wringer and are due for some good," Elaina said.

Angela squeezed her arm. "Let yourself love again."

They were right. She deserved to have someone in her

life who would be a willing partner and an attentive lover. Which she imagined Grayson would be.

"Thank you, ladies. You've helped me see things more clearly."

She spent the evening—and late into the night—thinking about her life. Now that she could see Hallie from Grayson's perspective, she knew her baby could benefit from early intervention, but JenniLynn was overwhelmed and not sure where to start. It would be so easy to rush to Grayson and ask him to fix her problems, but she'd promised that she would rely on herself first and foremost.

Her family's future was in her hands, and she had to decide what was best for them, and because she loved Grayson, what was best for him and Adam, too. He was too special to be someone's rebound, and until she was sure…

The next afternoon at work, Monica came out of her cozy office and sat down in the big leather chair across from JenniLynn. The expression on her assistant's face made her heart sink. Was she about to quit? "What's wrong?"

"Mayor Garrett…" Monica chewed on her lower lip. "I'm a good listener. If you want to tell me why you're so sad, maybe I can help. I couldn't help but notice that Mr. Abernathy has also been sad the last few days."

JenniLynn exhaled a big breath. "You're very observant. I could use your advice about something."

"Anything."

How could she bring up her concerns and not make it sound like she was saying there was something wrong with being on the spectrum? She twirled a lock of hair around her finger. "You've met my girls, and you've probably noticed Hallie's mannerisms."

"Yes, I have." Monica's smile was filled with understanding. "And I'm guessing that Mr. Abernathy noticed and said something?"

"Grayson suggested that I get an ASD evaluation for Hallie."

"Did that make you mad."

"No. It surprised me. I thought Hallie was just shy and that her regression was due to my divorce, but now I can see it." JenniLynn smiled at Monica. "Having you in my life has helped me realize that it will all be okay."

"Mayor Garrett, if it turns out that your daughter is neurodivergent, you are the perfect mother for Hallie. You have so easily made accommodations for me and made me feel so comfortable."

"I love hearing that. I'm so glad you like working with me."

"You even anticipate what I might need ahead of time. Like when you sent me back to the office when I needed a break from the Jobs Corps event." She leaned forward and rested her folded arms on the front of the big desk but didn't make eye contact. "You can tell me to mind my own business, but would you like to know what I think about you and Mr. Abernathy?"

"Yes, I would like to hear your opinion."

"You two make a good team. A happy team. I've watched the way you're encouraging and respectful of the other. He is so patient and kind, and I want to see you both happy again. My parents were so in love, and they always lived life to the fullest. Especially when my dad learned he had terminal cancer."

"Oh, Monica, I'm so sorry to hear that."

"You and Grayson remind me of them." Monica played with her pearl ring. "My mom always says, grab life while you can. Don't blink and miss the little moments."

A wave of tingles washed over JenniLynn's skin. Was fear keeping her from something that could be wonderful for her and her children? She glanced at her grandmother's clock, remembering one of her lessons with a similar message as her wise assistant's. "I think I understand."

Monica stood and smoothed her pink skirt. "Good. I'll get back to work." She paused in the doorway of her office. "If you want to leave a little bit early, I'll lock up on my way out at five."

"You read my mind." JenniLynn slipped on her shoes and stood. "Thank you for being so amazing."

"My pleasure," Monica said with a bright smile before disappearing into her cozy space.

Rather than wasting another minute, she decided to stop living in fear and start listening to the inner voice that was urging her toward her handsome neighbor.

At daycare, JenniLynn picked up Hallie first and then hurried to the room next door and motioned to her older two. "Let's go, girls. We have somewhere we need to be."

"Where are we going, Mommy?" Lila asked as she grabbed her backpack.

"We are going to see Grayson and Adam."

"Yay!" Sasha cheered, slung on her purple pack and took hold of her free hand. "Do you think they missed us?"

"I'm sure they did." At least she hoped so.

She got everyone buckled into their seats and started her car but then quickly realized she didn't know where Grayson was. He could be in Bronco for all she knew.

"What are we waiting on?" Lila asked.

"I have to find out where they are before I know where to go."

She turned up the radio to entertain the girls and typed

out a text message, hoping he would answer after all her days of ignoring him.

Where are you right now?

It would serve her right if he waited days to respond, but unlike him, she wouldn't be able to patiently sit by that long. He was the one in their relationship who had all the patience. She knew where he lived, and she would probably end up walking across the pastures and hopping over the barbed-wire fence if she had to.

Please don't let it be too late for us.

The dots appeared that told her he was typing, and her pulse raced as she waited.

I'm at home.

She responded immediately.

Can I come over?

I'll be here.

Yes! Time to go fight for my man.

She put the car in gear and headed for Ambling Hills Ranch. What she felt for Grayson was so much more than simple appreciation for his backup help as a single parent. He was not a rebound relationship. That had been a convenient excuse she'd told herself out of fear of risking her heart again.

Grayson Abernathy was so different from her ex. He was thoughtful and observant, noticing even the little things like how much dressing she liked on her salad. He was a man who only wanted the best for her and her children, which included looking out for Hallie. A man who had been so good about giving her all the time in the world to deal with her fears.

JenniLynn was so in love with Grayson, and sadly, she'd been putting him through hell. Would he give her one more chance to prove she was ready to love him the way he deserved?

Chapter Twenty-Two

Grayson was a complete wreck as he attempted to wear out the porch boards with the soles of his boots. He didn't know if he was waiting for the official end of his romance with JenniLynn or what could be the start of something amazing. Or just more waiting for her to be ready. That option was becoming harder with each passing day.

The sound of her car caught his attention, and he spun on his heels to go down into the front yard. Little hands were waving in the back seat, and that had to be a good sign. Surely she would not have brought the girls if this was going to be a bad conversation.

JenniLynn climbed out of her SUV, looking right at him with her lip caught between her teeth.

His heart seemed to pause, suspended in time, while he awaited what her expression meant and what would happen next.

A second later, her pretty mouth curved into a wide smile that made her eyes dance.

His inner sigh of relief went all the way to his bones, and he answered her smile with one of his own. He held back from what he really wanted to do, which was sweep her into his arms. Instead, he opened one of the back doors and helped Sasha out of her seat.

"What's going on, Miss Sasha?"

She threw her arms around his neck and gave him a big hug before he could put her down. "I missed you," she said.

"I missed you, too, honey." He set her on her feet, and she ran toward the gate to his backyard.

"I'm going to go see Moon Sparkle and Star Sparkle," she yelled over her shoulder.

Lila stepped out of the SUV. "Hi, Mr. Grayson."

"Hey there, Lila. Adam is in the backyard." He watched her run off.

JenniLynn came around to his side of the car with Hallie on her hip. The toddler reached for him, and he happily took her into his arms. "I missed you, Hallie girl."

She patted his cheeks and buried her face in his chest. "Miss you," she whispered and then wiggled in his arms. "Puppies?"

"Yes, you can go play with the puppies." He put her down, and she ran ahead of them to the backyard where the other kids could be heard laughing.

Finally he turned his full attention to JenniLynn. "I'm glad to see you, sweetheart. I missed you, too."

Her shoulders visibly relaxed. "That's good to hear."

"Did you think I wouldn't be glad to see you?"

"Well…" She dragged out the word as if searching for what to say and clasped her hands at her waist. "The thought did cross my mind. I rudely haven't answered your calls. Very unprofessional for a mayor, if I do say so myself."

That made him grin. "I think your tardiness in a response can be forgiven. At least you came in person."

"You've had the patience of a saint with me throughout our whole relationship. I've had a lot of chances, but…" She held her hands out to him, and he took hold of them.

"I'm hoping for one more chance to show you how much you mean to me."

"You've got it, sweetheart." He pulled her into an embrace and swayed with her under the shade of the trees with her peaches-and-sunshine scent filling his lungs.

"I couldn't see what you saw in Hallie," she said against his chest but then tipped up her face and held his gaze. "But I see it now, and I know everything is going to be okay and you were only doing what you truly thought was best for Hallie."

He bowed his head to kiss her softly. "I just want all four of you to have the best lives possible."

"My best life is the one that has you and Adam in it. Can you forgive me for running off on you?"

"There's nothing to forgive. That's what you do when you love someone."

A tear rolled down her cheek and across her sweet smile. "You love me?"

"Yes, I'm in love with you, and I'll wait as long as I have to if there is even a chance that you will someday feel the same way about me."

She cradled his cheek and brushed her mouth over his. "You don't have to wait, because I love you, too."

Their kiss was tender and bursting with the passion of new love, while children and dogs filled the background with a lovely kind of music. They whispered more sweet words until they were both assured they believed each other's love.

With their arms wrapped around each other's waists, they walked toward the backyard to join their children.

"I can't picture a future that you and Adam aren't a part of," JenniLynn said.

"I'm glad to hear you say that, because I got some fantastic news. Adam is going to be living with me full-time while his mom takes a job overseas."

"Oh, Grayson. That's amazing news. I can't tell you how happy I am for you. We need to celebrate."

"Which thing are we celebrating?"

"All of it," she said. "Adam staying. Our love. The amazing future we have ahead of us."

"I propose two different celebrations." He closed the gate behind them. "One that is a family event." He swept out his arm to encompass their whole rowdy bunch. "And another more private celebration that's just for you and me, Mayor Jenni."

"Brilliant idea. I propose I call in the babysitting favor I was promised. All four kids can be at my house, while we have a date night here at yours."

"We better seal that deal with a kiss." Since everyone in their families was okay with them being together, he leaned down to press his lips to hers.

"They're kissing!" Sasha yelled.

They both looked up to see the kids all giggling and smiling at them.

A couple of nights later, JenniLynn's friend Ella McIntyre came to spend the evening with the kids at her house. Ella was playing with the girls while JenniLynn put the finishing touches on her hair and makeup. She'd chosen to wear a silky soft wrap-dress in a soft shade of blue. Beneath, she wore her prettiest lingerie, and it made her feel beautiful. Or maybe it was due to the love bursting within her.

She went into the family room and performed a twirl to see if everyone approved of her outfit. She received a round of clapping and compliments.

Ella winked at her with a thumbs up. "You are going to knock his socks off."

Lila came over to touch the soft fabric. "You look so pretty, Mommy."

"Thank you, sweetie."

The doorbell rang, and she gave each girl a quick kiss then went to answer. Grayson and Adam were both standing there with big smiles and bouquets of fresh flowers in shades of pink. Love for both of them washed over her in a wave so big that she thought she might cry, but she turned it into a smile. "Those are so beautiful, and you both look very handsome tonight."

"Not as beautiful as you, sweetheart." Grayson's eyes swept her from head to toe. "Wow. You look gorgeous."

"Thank you." She accepted both bouquets.

"Have fun on your date," Adam said and headed into the house.

Grayson held out his hand. "Are you ready to go?"

"I am." With her flowers gathered in one arm, she laced her fingers with his as they walked to his truck.

He opened her door and stole a kiss before helping her up into the seat. Since he had already added a new gate, he drove through her ranch toward his. The ride was a bit on the bumpy side, and Grayson was talking about bringing in some gravel to improve it. They had started calling their private road Ambling Creek Drive, combining a word from each of their ranches.

Of course, Sasha called it Bling Creek and wanted Grayson to get sparkly rocks instead of plain old boring gravel. She had even suggested a truckload of glitter. She had not been happy when she found out that glitter would not be good for the cattle.

JenniLynn brought one of her bouquets to her nose and

inhaled the sweet fragrance. "I made the call, and Hallie has an appointment set up with an evaluator from early intervention."

"That's great, sweetheart. I'll be there to help you through all of it, every step of the way, when needed."

"I know you will. Have you heard back from your brother yet?"

"Yes. Jesse and Oscar are officially moving to Tenacity. They're going to build their own cabin on Ambling Hills."

"How exciting. I'm happy for all of you."

"Now, I just need to get the rest of our siblings to join us."

When they walked into his house, JenniLynn saw more flowers and candles ready to be lit. He went straight over to his stereo and turned on some music and then pulled a bottle of her favorite sparkling wine from a bucket of ice.

"Let's start with a toast to our long-awaited time alone."

She kicked off her high heels, knowing she didn't have to wear them to impress him. "That sounds like a lovely way to start the evening. I'll light the candles."

A few minutes later, her handsome cowboy handed her a glass of bubbly. "To us."

"To our love," she said. They clinked glasses, sipped and then she stood on her toes to taste the champagne on his lips.

"I have a gift for you. I found it in an antique store and couldn't resist." He pulled something from his shirt pocket. A long golden chain dangled from his fingers, and on the end was an antique watch pendant.

"Oh, Grayson, it's beautiful."

He set his glass on the coffee table and put the necklace over her head. "Since we both like clocks, it made me think of you."

"I love it. Thank you." The pendant rested near her heart, and she lifted it to get a closer look at the elegant watch face surrounded by clusters of tiny golden flowers. "I think it signifies how amazing you've been about giving me time. Time to figure things out and be ready. Is that what it means?"

He traced his finger along one edge of the golden chain, making her shiver. "It means that I'm going to do my best to show you the time of your life for the rest of mine."

"That's good, because I want to spend lots of time building something with you."

"Time is on our side," he said, and they both started laughing.

"I love that we can be silly together."

"Me, too. I like this kind of date night," he said. "I don't have to share you with anyone else, like I would have to do if we were at a restaurant."

She put down her glass and started unbuttoning his shirt. "It's just the two of us. All alone."

His grin widened, and he rolled each of his shoulders to help her take off his shirt. "What happens if I pull that little tie on the front of your dress?"

"Give it a tug and find out."

He did as she'd suggested, and her dress fell open to reveal her lacy pink lingerie. "Oh, sweetheart…"

His appreciative reaction emboldened her even more. "Worth the wait?"

"Absolutely, but I'm tired of waiting."

She let her dress flutter to the floor and hooked a finger around one of his beltloops. "Make love to me, cowboy."

"My pleasure, Mayor Jenni."

They didn't need fancy hotels or fine restaurants. All they needed was the glow of candlelight on bare skin and the love in one another's eyes. And time to build something beautiful.

Epilogue

"Grayson, you are not going to believe this," JenniLynn said as she rushed into her kitchen where he was stirring a pot of beans.

He chuckled. "From your level of excitement, I think I'm going to like it."

"You definitely are. I just got a call. At the dinosaur park dig they have started uncovering more bones."

"Are you kidding?"

"I'm not. I'm totally serious." She hugged him. "Do you want to turn off the stove and drive over there?"

"Heck yes. Let's load up the kids."

"Hey, Rowdy Bunch, we're going to the Dinosaur Center," she called to them. "Get your shoes on, please."

When they got to The Tenacity Dinosaur Center and Park, word had spread around town, and a crowd was starting to form behind a rope barrier. Since she was the mayor, she and Grayson went closer to the dig site to talk to the lead archaeologist, while the kids stayed back with Grayson's cousin Sage.

The archaeologist raised a hand to wave. "Good afternoon, Mayor Garrett."

"I hear you have made a new discovery."

The man's smile was wide and satisfied. "We certainly

have. So far we've uncovered a partial skeleton of a T. Rex, but that's not all. We have also uncovered some kimberlite."

JenniLynn grasped Grayson's arm. "Do you know what this means? This discovery all but guarantees the success of the Dinosaur Center and the reinvigoration of Tenacity's economy."

Grayson hugged her and lifted her off her feet. "This is amazing news for the whole town."

"Mayor Garrett," someone called to her. "Tell us what's going on."

They made their way over to the crowd so she could address everyone. "I have wonderful news for our town." She told them all about the T. Rex skeleton and the kimberlite. "For those of you who don't know about kimberlite, it's a rare and valuable type of igneous rock. It's valuable due to its rarity and the gems it protects. It will bring much needed funds to Tenacity."

"Do we have to share it with those rotten Bruckners?" someone asked.

"I'm glad someone asked about that." The chief of police joined her in front of the group. "Folks, I have some more news that will interest you. It concerns this land. Most of you will remember the Bruckners claimed that they owned it, but that is thankfully not true. After months of investigation that was being kept quiet by the Feds, the Bruckners have been arrested trying to pull a scam in South Dakota."

"What does that mean?" JenniLynn asked him.

"It means that they are con men," Chief Everett said, "and this land belongs to the town of Tenacity. Along with all of the profits."

Everyone started talking and hugging and cheering about the good news.

Grayson took her hand in his and flashed a big smile.

"Well, Mayor Jenni, it looks like you are getting this town cleaned up and back on its feet. It's time for a new era in Tenacity."

"It certainly is. One where we live happily ever after with our Rowdy Bunch."

Then Mayor JenniLynn Garrett kissed Grayson Abernathy right in front of the whole town.

And everyone cheered.

* * * * *

Get up to 4 Free Books!

We'll send you 2 free books from each series you try
PLUS a free Mystery Gift.

Both the **Harlequin® Special Edition** and **Harlequin® Heartwarming**™ series feature compelling novels filled with stories of love and strength where the bonds of friendship, family and community unite.

YES! Please send me 2 FREE novels from the Harlequin Special Edition or Harlequin Heartwarming series and my FREE Gift (gift is worth about $10 retail). I may cancel anytime by emailing ReaderServiceInfo@Harlequin.com or by calling 1-800-873-8635. If I don't cancel, I will receive 6 brand-new Harlequin Special Edition books every month and be billed just $6.39 each in the U.S. or $7.19 each in Canada, or 4 brand-new Harlequin Heartwarming Larger-Print books every month and be billed just $7.19 each in the U.S. or $7.99 each in Canada, a savings of 20% off the cover price. It's quite a bargain! Shipping and handling is just 75¢ per book in the U.S. and $1.75 per book in Canada.* I understand that accepting the free books and gift places me under no obligation to buy anything—they are mine to keep for free no matter what I decide.

Choose one:

☐ **Harlequin Special Edition** (235/335 BPA G3CD)

☐ **Harlequin Heartwarming Larger-Print** (161/361 BPA G3CD)

☐ **Or Try Both!** (235/335 & 161/361 BPA G3CE)

Name (please print)

Address   Apt. #

City   State/Province   Zip/Postal Code

Email: Please check this box ☐ if you would like to receive newsletters and promotional emails from Harlequin Enterprises ULC and its affiliates. You can unsubscribe anytime.

Mail to the **Harlequin Reader Service:**
IN U.S.A.: P.O. Box 1341, Buffalo, NY 14240-8531
IN CANADA: P.O. Box 603, Fort Erie, Ontario L2A 5X3

Want to explore our other series or interested in ebooks? Visit www.ReaderService.com or call 1-800-873-8635.

*Terms and prices subject to change without notice. Prices do not include sales taxes, which will be charged (if applicable) based on your state or country of residence. Canadian residents will be charged applicable taxes. Offer not valid in Quebec. This offer is limited to one order per household. Books received may not be as shown. Not valid for current subscribers to the Harlequin Special Edition or Harlequin Heartwarming series. All orders subject to approval. Credit or debit balances in a customer's account(s) may be offset by any other outstanding balance owed by or to the customer. Please allow 4 to 6 weeks for delivery. Offer available while quantities last.

Your Privacy — Your information is being collected by Harlequin Enterprises ULC, operating as Harlequin Reader Service. For a complete summary of the information we collect, how we use this information and to whom it is disclosed, please visit our privacy notice located at https://corporate.harlequin.com/privacy-notice. Notice to California Residents—Under California law, you have specific rights to control and access your data. For more information on these rights and how to exercise them, visit https://corporate.harlequin.com/california-privacy. For additional information for residents of other U.S. states that provide their residents with certain rights with respect to personal data, visit https://corporate.harlequin.com/other-state-residents-privacy-rights.

HSEHW2603